P9-DVQ-550

EDDIE RED
UNDERCOVER

SOLVE MORE MYSTERIES WITH EDDIE RED IN . . .

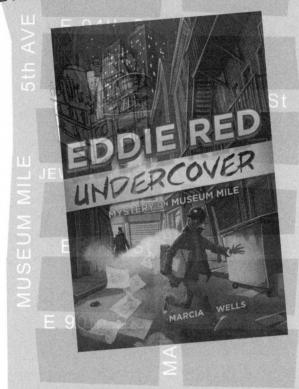

A Spring 2014 Kids' Indie Next Pick
A 2015 Edgar Awards Nominee

"A strong start to a promising new series, and as Eddie would say, it's über-cool." —*Booklist*

"[A] clever mystery." —*Publishers Weekly*

"Bound to be a series that will appeal to fans of fast-paced mysteries." —*School Library Journal*

E 95th St

E 94th St

E 91st St

E 90th S

E 89th St

E 88th St

E 86th St

CRIME DOESN'T TAKE A VACATION.

EDDIE RED
UNDERCOVER
MYSTERY IN MAYAN MEXICO

MARCIA WELLS

"All three kids are realistic and likable . . . [and] refreshingly, this book features an African American protagonist." —*School Library Journal*

"A fun whodunit. . . . Eddie's adventures are a good fit for older fans of Cam Jansen and Encyclopedia Brown." —*Booklist*

EDDIE RED
UNDERCOVER
DOOM AT GRANT'S TOMB

MARCIA WELLS

ILLUSTRATED BY MARCOS CALO

HOUGHTON MIFFLIN HARCOURT
BOSTON   NEW YORK

Copyright © 2016 by Marcia Wells
Illustrations copyright © 2016 by Marcos Calo

All rights reserved. For information about permission to reproduce
selections from this book, write to trade.permissions@hmhco.com or to
Permissions, Houghton Mifflin Harcourt Publishing Company,
3 Park Avenue, 19th floor, New York, New York 10016.

www.hmhco.com

The text was set in Adobe Garamond Pro.

Library of Congress Cataloging-in-Publication Data
Names: Wells, Marcia. | Calo, Marcos, illustrator.
Title: Doom at Grant's tomb / written by Marcia Wells ;
illustrated by Marcos Calo.
Description: Boston ; New York : Houghton Mifflin Harcourt, [2016] | Series:
Eddie Red undercover ; [3] | Summary: "Elusive art thief Lars Heinrich
returns to New York City looking to settle a score. Super sleuth
seventh-grader Edmund Xavier Lonrrot will need not only his photographic
mind and artistic talents, but any skill he possesses with cracking codes
as a string of the city's historical monuments become potential clues in
what could become one of the greatest heists in history."
—Provided by publisher.
Identifiers: LCCN 2015018547 | ISBN 9780544582606 hardcover
Subjects: | CYAC: Ciphers—Fiction. | Drawing—Fiction. | Memory—Fiction. |
Art thefts—Fiction. | Stealing—Fiction. | New York (N.Y.)—Fiction. |
Mystery and detective stories. | BISAC: JUVENILE FICTION / Mysteries &
Detective Stories. | JUVENILE FICTION / People & Places / United States /
Native American. | JUVENILE FICTION / Action & Adventure / General.
Classification: LCC PZ7.W4663 Do 2016 | DDC [Fic]—dc23 LC record avail-
able at http://lccn.loc.gov/2015018547

Manufactured in the United States of America
DOC 10 9 8 7 6 5 4 3 2 1
4500581400

For Team Eddie:
Ben, Ann, Kristin, Beth,
and of course
my mom

EDDIE RED
UNDERCOVER

Chapter 1

BOOM

———

10:42 A.M., MONDAY

The first bomb arrived the week before my twelfth birthday.

It was delivered to the police station on a Monday, in a brown package. They told me the whole block shut down for a solid hour until the bomb squad determined that it was a dummy. The worst part is that there was a note taped to the side:

1 — Eddie will know what this means

"I have *no* idea what this means," I say for the millionth time. I'm sitting in a hard wooden chair in Chief Williams's office. The chief sits across from me, tapping a pencil on his desk. He's the man in charge who hired me eight months ago. A stern-looking man, but a nice one. He waited a week to call me in. Happy birthday to me.

"There must be other people named Eddie in the department," I add. "An Edward, maybe?"

"We're looking into it" is the chief's only reply.

Last spring I worked for the NYPD because of my photographic memory and ability to draw almost perfect character sketches. They gave me the code name Eddie Red and had me stake out some of New York's most important art museums. Despite being kept in the dark about the real guts of the operation, I managed to stop the international art thief Lars Heinrich before he carried out a major robbery. Unfortunately Lars took off before the police could capture him.

I thought my life would go back to normal, but here I am, right back in the hot seat. I stare at the so-called bomb in front of me. It's a digital clock with bomb wiring and a timer that flashes 24:11 over and over again. My mind starts snapping pictures as I try to understand what this all means. *Click*—green wires poking out of the back in a coiled twist. *Click*—the Eddie note scribbled in red ink. *Click*—a white lump of explosives wrapped in clear plastic.

Detective Bovano clears his throat behind me. He hasn't said much since I arrived, just sort of hovered by the door like a dark fog. He's lost some weight since I last saw him. I heard he won a medal for exemplary police work—a.k.a. getting shot while protecting me.

"Have you ever heard of the IRA?" Bovano asks.

"Uh . . ." I search my brain. "Is that the group that collects people's taxes?"

They both chuckle and the tension in the room deflates. They're laughing at me as if I'm a dumb kid.

"That's the IRS." Chief Williams rubs the back of his neck. "The IRA stands for the Irish Republican Army. They're a terrorist group that fights to make Ireland an independent republic. One of their operatives from the nineties, a fellow named Patrick O'Malley, built bombs just like this one." He shifts forward and touches the frayed ends of the wires with a pencil. "His calling card is this twist of green wires. The luck of the Irish." He removes his hand quickly, as if the bomb just stung him. "This bag of white clay was attached to the wires, made to look like the explosive C-4. Our forensics lab tells us the clay is actually gluten-free baking flour mixed with water. Does that mean anything to you?"

I shake my head. This is getting stranger by the second.

The chief opens a file and pulls out a mug shot of a middle-aged man. "Here's our latest picture of O'Malley. Do you recognize him in that filing system of yours?" He taps his forehead.

I glance at the picture, mentally noting all the details so I can draw them later. O'Malley is a bit heavy, with saggy skin and a receding hairline. Everything about him is gray: gray clothing, gray hair, gray eyes. The date on the picture reads 1994, so I'm guessing he'd be in his seventies now. "No, sir," I say.

"Well, it was worth a shot." He puts the picture away, slides on a pair of latex gloves, and gently places the bomb in a blue evidence bin. "I don't want you to worry about this. We think the Eddie note is just a coincidence." He snaps off the gloves and shoots me a meaningful look. "No need to worry your parents, either."

I nod. There's *no* way I would tell my parents about this. Mom would have us signed up in a witness protection program faster than you can say *Moving to Australia.*

"What about Lars?" I ask. "Did your men find any record of him in New York?" I open my art pad and hold up the picture I drew of Lars Heinrich. I saw him a month ago in the airport when I was coming back from a vacation in Mexico. Judging from his sneer and the way he narrowed his eyes at me, he knew exactly who I was, and was very angry. It's not a good combination.

A terrible thought occurs to me. "What if *he* was the one who sent the bomb? He definitely knows who I am. What if—?"

"No," Bovano interrupts. "This is O'Malley's work. And I already told you, Lars never knew you existed. I questioned his gang members myself. I have a built-in lie detector." He points to his temple. "Hasn't failed me yet."

Considering I lied to him for a solid four months when we worked together, I'd say his detector needs a tune-up. "But—"

"O'Malley always works alone," the chief adds gently. "And Lars was seen entering Germany two weeks ago. He's not in New York. You're safe." He glances at Bovano, then quickly looks away. Warning bells sound in my head. They're not telling me the whole story.

The chief shuffles through some papers on his desk. "We need your help on another matter. There was a high-profile jewel robbery last week. We're worried the thieves' next target might be a diamond exhibit

LARS

coming to the Met. I already spoke to your parents about hiring you for surveillance work. Does twenty dollars an hour sound good?"

They want me back on the force? Really? "Okay," I say. I should be thrilled about this, but I can't shake the feeling that something's not adding up.

"Frank, get Eddie here another contract," the chief instructs Bovano. "Short term." He stands up and puts on his navy blue jacket, part of his chief's uniform. "Your mother made me promise you wouldn't be out in the field. You'll be stationed in a surveillance van." He smiles. "She drives a hard bargain."

If Mom agreed to this, we must really need the money. Dad still doesn't have a full-time job, and Senate Academy (my private school for gifted kids) is expensive. The police are paying my tuition this year as part of my reward for stopping the art heist, but I still have to buy books and supplies.

I stand up. "If I solve this case, will you pay for Senate again next year? Or maybe hire me on full time? You know — salary, benefits, all that stuff?"

The chief blinks. "We'll see. There are tight budget restrictions." He shakes my hand. "Good to have you back, Eddie. Detective Bovano will contact you in a few days. I trust you know your way to the elevator?"

I nod and slowly leave the office, closing the door behind me. Walking past the familiar rows of desks and ringing phones and busy cops, I position myself by the water cooler and pull out my art pad while I wait for Detective Bovano. He was my partner last year, and I want to talk to him about the case. No time like the present.

While I wait, I sketch a picture of O'Malley, remembering how his long nose ended in a point, how the skin bagged beneath his eyes. He looks older than Lars—of course, Lars has had a ton of plastic surgery, so I can't be sure. Could they have met? Do bad guys get together over bagels and coffee to chat about evil plots together?

Bovano walks out of the office and down the hallway. He doesn't see me.

I snap my art pad shut and call out, "Sir! Detective Bovano!" I catch up to him by the elevator.

He presses the Up button with his thumb, and frowns. "What are you still doing here?" His bushy eyebrows move up and down as he scrutinizes me.

"I was thirsty." I point to the water cooler over my shoulder. "I thought we could chat about the case. It seems like you guys aren't telling me everything. I can handle the truth, Detective. Are Lars and O'Malley working together? And I'd like to know more about the jewel robbery. We should meet about this, discuss possible theories." Last year Bovano and I had our differences, but in the end we sort of bonded (stressful alleyway shootouts tend to bring people together). I think he'll be more open to working with me this time.

"No." The elevator door opens and he steps inside, holding a hand up to block me from entering. "Take the next one. I'm going up."

"Just tell me," I practically shout. "What if Lars and O'Malley are working together?"

Bovano doesn't respond, just shakes his head and looks away. As the door swooshes shut, I swear he whispers one word:

"Boom."

Chapter 2

MR. FRANK

7:48 A.M., TUESDAY

"No way," I say to my father the next morning. I drop my backpack on the floor for emphasis. "I am *not* starting seventh grade with a babysitter." Dad just informed me that I am to have a police escort to and from school "as a safety precaution only."

Dad scratches his mustache. "Look, your mom and I just want you safe until this Lars fellow is caught. The police say he's in Germany, but what if he returns to the city? An escort is a good idea. I'd take you to school myself but—"

I gasp. "This was *your* idea?" No wonder my mom was acting nervous before she left for work this morning. She knew I'd be upset.

"Not entirely. We simply voiced concern about your safety. The chief thought that an escort was the best course of action."

I guess I don't blame my parents for being worried about Lars. He's wanted in at least five countries for grand theft, fraud, and assault. I read in the newspaper that he's cost those governments more than thirty million dollars in stolen goods. Infamous for leaving clues that create geometric patterns on a map, he plays games with the police while setting his sights on the city's treasure. He's cold and ruthless and obsessed with winning. Last year I stopped him from stealing some priceless paintings by Picasso. As far as I know, I'm the only person who's ever ruined his evil plans.

I shake my head. "If you're so worried, why are you letting me work with the cops again?"

Dad smiles. "We're proud of the work you've done on the force. And you'll be safe in the surveillance van. No place safer, I imagine." He pats me on the shoulder. "This is no big deal. Either you cooperate or Mom moves us to Canada. You know she will."

"Fine." Smelling defeat, I grab my backpack off the floor.

"Wait," Dad says. "I need to take a picture. Your first day of middle school, I can't believe it." He pulls out his phone and snaps a quick shot.

"Just don't take a picture of my escort," I mutter.

Knowing Dad, he'd post it on Facebook and blow our cover the first day.

I open the door to our apartment, prepared to jog down the stairs and meet my police contact on the sidewalk. A woman is standing in the hallway, adjusting the front of her black dress as if she's uncomfortable wearing girly things. She's got dark caramel skin, long curly black hair, and huge brown eyes that are speckled with gold. The word *goddess* comes to mind.

"Oh," Dad says. "Hi. I mean, hello. G-good morning," he stammers. I go for a much smoother approach by grinning and waving at her like an excited first-grader.

She tilts her head and blinks her golden eyes at me. "Hi, Eddie," she says in a soft southern accent. "I'm your new Aunt Paula."

An hour later, I'm sitting in art class, the first class period of the day. "I can't believe you have a bodyguard," my best friend, Jonah, whispers. "You never used to need a bodyguard. Why now?" His foot taps so hard, it bounces the curly red hair on his head.

"I don't know, but I'm going to find out." I straighten my glasses. "At least Paula's nice. She's supposed to be my mother's sister who just moved to the city and has some 'free time'"—I air-quote the words—"to take me to and from school. She'll be here this afternoon. You can meet her if you want."

"Do you think she's FBI?" he asks. "I bet she has a lot of cool weapons."

I shrug. "She didn't say."

When I took the bus with Paula, she told me she's from a southern state that cannot be named, working for a government agency that cannot be named, and I'm pretty sure her real name's not Paula, either. It was a strange conversation of noninformation, but she's smart and funny and I think our arrangement is going to work out just fine.

Our art teacher, Mrs. Smith, claps twice to get our attention. "Take your seats, everyone," she says. "You'll find a fresh canvas and paints under each desk. I'd like you to paint how you feel right now." She points to a big color chart on the wall. "What do the colors say to you? Yellow for an imaginative mood? Blue for relaxed? It can be totally abstract. It's up to you."

Jonah scampers to his spot four seats over, which is for the best. I'll never get any work done if he's beside me. Lately he's been obsessed with the cartoon *Walter the Flying Cow*, so when he giggles and grabs two jars of black and white paint, I know where he's headed.

It's a new year, a new classroom, even a new section of the school. The seventh- and eighth-graders make up the middle school of Senate Academy, and we have a whole wing of the building to ourselves. It was remodeled a year ago so everything is new and über-fancy.

I crack open a bottle of red. I am bold today. Adventurous. I am Eddie Red, and I am invincible. I streak thick red lines across the canvas, then dab some orange in the middle. The rest of the class is chatting in a quiet hum, the slightly sweet smell of paint in the air.

"Okay, quiet down, people," Mrs. Smith says after about ten minutes. "According to an email I just received, there will be a new student teacher this fall. He's due to arrive any minute."

Student teachers have a weird history here at Senate. Legend has it that one guy who taught senior math made the kids eat a pickled herring (a gross fish in a jar) whenever they came late to class. And about five years ago, another teacher named Rita Renson fed her seventh-graders candy and let them wrestle in the classroom. She got busted after a kid broke his nose.

There's a knock on the door. "That must be him," Mrs. Smith says. "Please welcome Mr. Frank."

The door opens. A familiar heavy-set figure with bushy eyebrows and sagging jowls is standing in the doorway. His dark eyes sweep the room until they settle on me. His nose wrinkles as if he smells bad cheese.

And my seventh grade year is officially ruined.

Chapter 3

THE FIGHTING TROJANS

___

3:20 P.M., SAME DAY

All day long I smile and laugh and pretend to be the happy kid who's back in school with his buddies, but my mind keeps repeating: *Why is Detective Frank Bovano a teacher at my school? Why? Why? Why?* My performance is Oscar-worthy. During lunch I send my mom three angry texts demanding she tell me why she decided to destroy my life. She writes back and promises she never requested in-school protection. Which means my instincts are correct: The police are *definitely* hiding something.

After school I attend my first-ever student council meeting. Last spring I was elected class representative, along with Jonah and two other kids, although

Jonah's not here today because he's got Hebrew lessons. He's studying for his bar mitzvah later this year.

I haven't told Jonah about Mr. Frank's true identity. I wanted to a thousand times today, but decided I'll call him tonight. Jonah is 100 percent trustworthy, but if you surprise him with big news, he's about as subtle as a grenade.

The council meeting is in Señora Luna's Spanish classroom. I walk in and take a seat in the back. My head is up, my mouth is smiling, and I am numb. Mr. Frank is already up front, leaning against the whiteboard. He glances at me, then looks away, pretending not to watch my every move. It's been like this all day. He has come to every single one of my classes, and even ate near me during lunch. At one point in math class I had to go to the bathroom and he started to follow me in, then realized what he was doing and stationed himself outside the door.

I've studied him all day long, trying to figure out what he's up to. He's wearing a horrid teacher outfit, complete with a collared shirt, an ugly plaid tie, a swampy-green-colored sweater, and brown slacks that are a size too small. I drew a picture of him during second-period study hall. There's a subtle lump be-

MR. FRANK

neath his sweater on the left side. It's a gun, I'm sure of it. And then in Spanish class he was bending forward to help a student conjugate a verb when I noticed a faint circle in his back pocket, suspiciously resembling handcuffs. Handcuffs and a gun? What exactly does he think's going to happen here at Senate?

A few other kids from my class fill in the seats around me. Jenny Miller, the girl I've had a crush on since last year, slides into the chair next to mine and my pulse kicks up a notch. She pulls out a thick notebook with color-coded tabs and flips to the orange section, then fishes an orange pen out of her bag. She's our class secretary and is known for her killer organizational skills.

I try to look like I'm going to take important notes, fumble my pencil, and drop it. It rolls three desks away.

Jenny hands me a new pencil. It's white with the word TUESDAY printed in blue letters. Today is Tuesday. Like I said, she's über-organized.

The president of the eighth grade class, Mateo González, bangs a gavel on a desk and calls the meeting to order. "Welcome, new members," he says. "We're going to get right to it. We have two goals this fall. The first is the Fall Carnival, organized by the seventh grade." He waves his gavel in our general direction. "You have three weeks to prepare. As you know, the carnival raises money for our second goal, the Homecoming parade float."

A few kids hoot and pump their fists in the air. "Homecoming is in October," Mateo continues. "We'll be building a Trojan horse." More hoots. Someone yells, "Go Trojans!" Our school's mascot is the Fighting Trojans, so there are cartoon drawings of guys in ancient armor hanging on banners all over the hallways. Don't ask me what ancient Greeks have to do with New York City geeks.

Jenny touches my hand and I just about fall out of my chair. She hands me a folded piece of paper.

A note from Jenny Miller? Do I open it now? Later? What if it says something like *You have spinach in your teeth* and I don't open it and then I walk around with spinach in my teeth all afternoon?

I unfold the paper. Disappointment washes over me. It's from Milton Edwards. I'd recognize his blocky handwriting anywhere. The six words printed on the page send my head reeling:

HOW DO YOU KNOW DETECTIVE BOVANO?

I look over at Milton, who's sitting three seats away. His intense stare pins me like a bug under a microscope. How does *he* know Detective Bovano? Milton's a nice kid who I've known since kindergarten, but we've never been close friends. He speaks in lists and has an odd obsession with condiments. Right now he's wearing a T-shirt with salt and pepper shakers on it that says SHAKE IT UP!, and last year he brought in a book called *The History of Mustard.*

Suddenly I remember him mentioning that his mom is a scientist and sometimes does forensic work for the NYPD. I glance at Bovano, who is currently scowling in Milton's direction. This is a complication I don't need.

Cheeks burning, I stare at the desk for the rest of the meeting, not hearing a single word about the school carnival or the Trojan horse. After the meeting ends, I hang out in the back of the room and pretend to read the Spanish posters about lunch foods: ME GUSTA UN SANDWICH, ¿TE GUSTA UN SANDWICH? Once everyone's gone, I tiptoe down the quiet hall. Just two rows of lockers separate me from the front door. I need time alone to figure out what to say to Milton. And Paula said she'd be waiting for me on the steps, so that's a plus.

"Well?" Milton's loud and rather obnoxious voice echoes around me. He steps out from the shadows of the front office.

"I don't know what you're talking about." I try to walk past him, but he grabs my arm and pulls me down the hall, away from the freedom of daylight.

"First of all," he says, "you looked like you swallowed a frog when Mr. Frank walked into art class this morning. Second, he's watched you all day like he knows you. Third, you've been really twitchy, like you're nervous about something. Fourth—"

"Okay, I get it." Before I can come up with a lame excuse for my nervous behavior, large hands grab us by the collar and yank us backwards into a small room. The door clicks shut and we're plunged into darkness. The smell of soapy peppermint surrounds me, and I realize we've been stuffed into the janitor's supply closet.

The light clicks on. "Do we have a problem here, boys?" Bovano says.

"No, sir," Milton squeaks. "It's just . . . I know you. You're Detective Bovano. My mom works with Casey Weston in forensics and I met you at Casey's barbecue last year. My name is Milton Edwards."

Bovano furrows his bushy lie-detector eyebrows,

squinting as if trying to place Milton's face. "Right," he says in a tight voice. "Now I remember."

"Are you working undercover, sir?" Milton's voice falls to a hush. "I won't tell anyone. I was just asking Edmund about it because first of all, it seems like he knows you, and second—"

Bovano puts a big hand up to silence him. "I do know Edmund," he admits. "I went to college with his father. I'm here because we suspect the mob is laundering money through the school. I can count on you to keep this quiet, can't I?"

Milton nods, his almond-shaped eyes growing wider. His mom is Japanese, and his dad's blond, so he has an unusual combination of sandy hair and blue eyes that are tapered at the corners. His nose is long and slightly bent to the left. Details I notice when I'm smooshed between him and a bottle of floor cleaner.

Bovano leans in like he's about to tell us a big, important secret. The garlic bread they served us at lunch today isn't doing his breath any favors. "Maybe you can help us," he says. "I'll talk to your mother. In the meantime, keep your ear to the ground. Let me know if you hear anything suspicious. Kids talking about their dads' new cars, things like that. Okay?"

Milton nods again. "Awesome," he whispers. "I promise I won't say a word."

Bovano smiles and opens the door. "I need to speak with Edmund here about a birthday surprise I'm planning for his dad," he says. "Run along now, Milton. I'll expect your report next week."

Milton grins and trots down the hallway. And I'm left alone with Mr. Frank/Detective Bovano/my father's new best buddy.

Bovano sighs. "Can we trust him not to blow this?"

I'm shocked he's asking me a question instead of barking an order. "Yes," I say. "He's trustworthy." I may not know Milton super well, but I do know this: When I peed my pants on the playground in first grade, he was the one who took me to the nurse's office for a change of clothes. He never told anyone what happened, never teased me about it.

Bovano and I stand there a moment, not speaking. I stare at his face, at the stress lines by his eyes and mouth. Why is he here guarding me at Senate? If the police feel I need this much protection, then Lars must be in New York, or at least headed this way. Is Lars working with O'Malley? I need more information, but I know Bovano won't tell me anything. Maybe I'll sneak into his office and go through his papers like I did last year. The thought makes me queasy.

He sighs again and motions for me to follow him to the front door. "I want you to know that this bodyguard job was not my idea. But the chief wants you protected until Heinrich is caught, so here I am. In the meantime, keep your head down and your mouth shut. Understood?"

We reach the main doors and he turns left, presumably to head back to whatever classroom the school has assigned him as home base. He stomps away, not bothering to wait for my reply.

"And don't forget to do your homework," he tosses over his shoulder.

Chapter 4

PEPPER

—————

3:28 P.M., THURSDAY

"Let's go over what we know," I say to Jonah two days later. We're having an afternoon snack at Mario's Pizzeria. It's a small, cramped restaurant with only three tables, but it's got the best pizza in the city. The secret is the double cheese, double sauce.

Paula is sitting over by the window. I told her that Jonah and I need to work on an English assignment together, so she agreed to escort us here. She's reading a magazine and watching the door every few minutes. She's only ten feet away, but with the loud radio playing eighties music, the *whoosh* of the pizza oven being opened and closed, and a cook answering the phone yelling, "Mario's! We bake 'em, you take 'em!," there's no way she can hear our conversation.

I pull out my list of strange things that have happened this past week. Are they clues to one case or a bunch of separate cases? Or not clues at all?

* A fake bomb
* Time on fake bomb — 24:11
* Note in RED ink: "1 — Eddie will know what this means"
* Lars Heinrich — Germany
* O'Malley — Ireland
* Diamonds at Met
* Recent jewel robbery — what and where?
* Bodyguards for Edmund

"It's a weird list," I say.

"Very." Jonah smears another glob of peanut butter on his red pepper pizza and takes a bite. He glances over at Paula. "Do you think she needs some water? Her glass looks low."

I roll my eyes. Of *course* he's smitten with her. "She's fine. Don't engage her in conversation. We can't snoop on the police if we're hanging out with the police, remember?" I don't mention that yesterday I gave her a picture that I drew of her as a thank-you for protecting me. I think she liked it. She smiled the whole way to school.

PAULA

He shrugs and pops the last bite of pizza into his mouth. "When's Milton supposed to call?" he says in a sticky voice.

"Any minute now." Milton is currently checking his mom's computer for the latest police reports. She receives a weekly email that contains updates on crimes around the city. It's the perfect solution to spying on Bovano. I told Milton we'd form a secret "police squad club" to help solve Bovano's case, and then maybe the cops would hire us as kid agents. I feel bad for lying to him and using him for information, but duty calls.

I check to make sure my phone is on. My parents got me a "new" iPhone for school. Translation: I get to use my mom's old one and *she* got a new one. It's great except it has way too many goofy pictures of my dad—wearing a napkin on his head at a fancy restaurant, twirling his mustache while sipping tea at a coffee shop—not to mention a few barfy selfies of the two of them kissing. I can't delete any of them until Mom finishes her photo albums, which may take all year.

I fiddle with the phone. I hate waiting. I wish I could go over to Milton's house and look at the files personally, but he said his mom is home and doesn't

EDDIE BOMB

like other kids messing around with her computer. I sigh and flip open my art pad, studying the picture I drew of the bomb. The Eddie note is so creepy. It taunts me and my lack of detective skills.

Tap-tap-tap. Jonah taps his pencil on the table. "Lars loves maps and puzzles. What could the time 24:11 mean? Is it coordinates on a map? What's on Twenty-Fourth and Eleventh?" He types something into his laptop. "That's near the Hudson River. Oh, there's an art gallery on the corner. Check it out."

He turns the computer toward me but stops halfway when his phone starts to vibrate, sending tremors across the table and onto my arms. He frowns. "It's Milton. I guess he got confused and called me by accident."

"Let's hope he doesn't get *too* confused," I mutter. We need his focus to be razor sharp.

Jonah grabs my notebook, picks up the phone, and says, "Talk to me." It's the strangest one-sided conversation I've ever heard:

"Uh-huh. Crown jewels? Whoa. Yeah, I got it — emeralds, sapphires, diamonds. Really? Ireland?" Jonah's eyes flicker to mine and he raises an eyebrow. "Yep. Cleopatra, like the queen? Oh. Wait, but that's—" He shifts the phone in his hand and hunches over the notebook. I can't see what he's writing. "The tomb, like the *actual* tomb? No. All right. Yep. Yep. William who? The gold one? No, I don't remember. Oh. That's all?" He looks disappointed.

We told Milton that we overheard Bovano talking on the phone about a bomb and a jewel robbery, and asked that he look through his mom's reports for anything mentioning the words "bomb" or "jewels." Pretty close to the actual truth, but I trust Milton to keep his mouth shut.

Jonah taps the pencil like a drum and says, "Good work, soldier. We'll report back tomorrow." With that, he hangs up.

"Well?" I say.

He shows me his notes. "Two interesting things. Well, five interesting things, but two categories. First, there's been an increase in security around a bunch of city landmarks."

LANDMARKS
1—Cleopatra's Needle—in CP
  (Central Park)
2—Grant's Tomb

3—William Sherman the gold dude—
    in CP
4—Penn Station

I scratch my head. "William Sherman the gold dude?"

"There's a statue in Central Park of some guy named William. The statue is gilded. You know, covered in gold? Milton says we went there on a class trip in third grade. I must have been sick that day, 'cause I have no idea what he's talking about."

I flip through images in my mind. A statue covered in gold? I'm not seeing it.

I know the other landmarks, though. Cleopatra's Needle is a huge obelisk from ancient Egypt that sits in Central Park, and Grant's Tomb is a memorial to the Civil War hero General Ulysses Grant. It's just outside of Manhattan, while Penn Station is in Midtown and is one of the busiest and most famous train stations in the world.

I'm failing to see any connection between these sites. "Another weird list," I say, dipping my pizza crust into the ranch dressing we ordered.

Jonah nods while typing something into his computer. "Milton said that the monuments have been labeled as a terrorist alert. No mention of the word 'bomb,' but that's what terrorists usually use, right? The sites could be connected with your Eddie bomb."

"The timing works." I stare at the list. If Lars is in town, and if he's working with O'Malley, then these sites are not random. Everything is intentional with Lars. He loves to play with the police and send them hidden messages.

Jonah takes another bite of pizza, still typing away on his computer. "Anyway, the second interesting thing is about the Duchess of Ireland. She's in New York this month for cultural events, diplomatic meetings, stuff like that. There was a fancy fundraiser banquet she was supposed to attend last week. Her crown was being delivered to her in an armored car when it was hijacked on Fifth Avenue. No one was hurt but the crown is gone. Oh, check it out. Here she is." He turns the screen around to show me. "I didn't know Europe still has duchesses, but apparently they do."

I expect to see an elderly lady in a frilly evening gown, but instead there are a bunch of pictures of a young woman, maybe early thirties, wearing a crisp navy business suit. She has high cheekbones and brown hair, with intelligent blue eyes. She's mostly pictured shaking hands with different world leaders, but in a few she's in a more formal gown with a small but beautiful crown on top of her head. It's made of several rows of diamonds that twist in a way that reminds me of a wreath, curving into a heart in the center, where a large emerald sits flanked by blue sapphires.

I give a low whistle. "That's some crown. She must be pretty upset."

Jonah pulls out a thick city map from his bag. "Yeah. Her and anyone else with money coming to the city. No wonder the police hired you again. I bet the Met is freaking out about their upcoming diamond exhibit, especially since they're on Fifth Avenue, right where the robbery went down."

"This must be the high-profile robbery that Chief Williams told me about," I add. But if this is the handiwork of Lars, why would he steal a crown? He loves art, not jewels.

Jonah nods and pushes the computer closer to me. "Will you draw the crown? Just a rough sketch?"

"Sure." I flip my art pad to a fresh page and start sketching. The design isn't complicated, but there are a *lot* of diamonds.

"I'm going to look up these landmarks," he says.

THE CROWN OF THE
DUCHESS OF IRELAND

"Maybe their locations are significant." He frowns. "According to the map, there are no monuments over by Eleventh and Twenty-Fourth. Are we reading too much into the time on the bomb?"

I shrug and keep sketching. All we have are more questions and zero answers. Are Lars and O'Malley working together? If they are, did they steal the crown? O'Malley is from Ireland and the duchess is from Ireland. Is that important?

The more I think about all the different puzzle pieces, the more they become a tangled mess of nonsense in my brain. My arm starts to cramp up from drawing the little looping jewels.

"What's wrong?" Jonah demands.

After resting my pencil down on the table, I stretch my fingers and glance over at Paula. She's eating one of Mario's famous fudge brownies. She smiles and gives me a quick wink, then turns the page of her magazine.

"I feel like there's a secret plan I don't know about," I say. "Why would the police give me protection if Lars is supposedly back in Germany? I feel like they're using me as bait, like *I'm* the worm on the hook and they're trying to catch the big Lars fish."

Jonah snorts. "Don't be ridiculous. They'd never

use you as bait. It's highly illegal. They're just being careful. You work for the police, and they take care of their own."

I sigh and look down at my art pad. I guess the drawing of the crown came out okay.

Jonah snaps his fingers. "I almost forgot." He unzips a pouch on his backpack and pulls out a slim black box. "Your birthday present finally came in the mail. Happy birthday." He hands me the box. He was going to come over three days ago for cake and ice cream, but between school starting the next day and the police calling me down to the station, our plans for a birthday party fizzled.

I smile. "Thanks." I pop open the lid. A pen sits nestled in white tissue paper. It's dark blue and about half the size of a regular pen. He knows I love to draw, so maybe it's a special kind of draft pen. I pick it up to examine it. Seems pretty regular to me. "A pen?" I ask.

He grins and his leg starts twitching, bumping the sides of the table and making our plastic cups rattle. "Not just a pen. A *pepper* pen. It's filled with pepper spray, an excellent weapon for today's student."

I drop it back in the box as if it just burned me. He's given me a lot of strange gifts in the past — a rubber nose with candy boogers in it, a fart machine that killed all the plants in our apartment—but this is different. This is a semi-dangerous weapon.

He grabs it and uncaps one end. "Look, it even writes." He demonstrates on my notepad by writing *Jonah is cool* in blue ink. "The other end is filled with pepper spray. One shot to someone's eyes will blind them for at least ten minutes. Just flip the safety switch off and press this button." He points to a tiny red knob on the end of the pen. "Keep it in your pocket. In case."

Sweat springs up on my forehead. "In case what?" Is it me, or is it suddenly very warm in here?

"You know." He clicks the cap back on and shoves the pen into my hand.

I stare at him blankly, so he leans forward, glancing around to make sure no one's listening.

"In case you're bait," he whispers.

Chapter 5

LITTLE RED

────

TWENTY MINUTES LATER

Fat drops of rain are splattering the sidewalk when we leave the restaurant. Jonah clutches his computer bag to his chest and sprints down the block to his parents' dental office, waving goodbye over his shoulder. That kid is like a vampire in sunlight when it comes to rain on his tech gear.

Paula steps off the curb and whistles loudly for a cab. Clearly she doesn't understand how nuts New York gets in the rain. "No taxi's going to stop," I tell her. "They're all occupied." Three cabs drive by with their service lights switched off, as if to illustrate my point. "The subway's a block away. Just four stops to my house."

She waves me off. "No subways." She holds a hand out for another taxi. Occupied.

No subways? Why? More cars pass. One hits a

puddle and sends water spraying over Paula's black skirt and jean jacket. Cursing softly, she pulls out a Kleenex and dabs at her clothes. After eight more cabs go by, she gives up. "Fine," she grumbles. "We'll take the subway."

If the streets are wet, the subway steps are even wetter. We hold on to the rail so we don't slip, and carefully make our way through the press of soggy people trying to get home. I hear Paula mutter about "rude New Yorkers" and "cold northern weather." It's rush hour, and the station is extra jammed because of the rain. There's a swampy smell in the air, a combination of pee, body odor, and bubblegum.

She grabs my hand as we struggle toward our platform. She seems nervous. Maybe she's claustrophobic and hates crowds. I lead the way, weaving expertly through the sea of bodies. A group of obnoxious teens knocks into us. Paula shoots them a look that could melt steel. Yep, she definitely hates crowds.

Our train arrives and we board, pushing our way into the corner of the subway car. Just four stops until we can exit. The doors ding and snap closed. With a jerking rumble, the train starts to move, swaying as it picks up speed. Suddenly the emergency brakes slam on and we all stumble forward. I catch myself on a metal pole before I fall.

Crrrrunch! The car jolts hard, sending us flying for real this time. I fall down on my knees and am about to hit my head when Paula jerks me to her side with an iron grip. "Hold on!" she shouts. "We just hit something!"

What? Through my confusion, a panicked thought strikes: What if Lars followed me down here and is attacking the train? I hold my breath. No fire, no flashes of light from an exploding bomb. I become aware that Paula's arm is covering my head, squishing my cheek against the dirty floor.

"Stay down," she commands. Her usually smiling face has morphed into the serious expression of a warrior as she looks back and forth, back and forth. Her hand is inside her jacket. I catch a flash of black. She's got a gun in there!

The train groans and the lights flicker. "Sorry, folks," the conductor says, his voice tinny over the loudspeaker. "An old I-beam fell onto the tracks and we sideswiped it. I'm going to need everyone to vacate at the next station. Attendants will be there to assist you."

Some passengers complain but others are helping people off the floor and murmuring words of comfort. Even the group of pushy kids who bumped into us is helping an old man get back to his seat.

Paula's still smothering me. Her arm is heavy and the floor smells like stale nachos and sweat socks and I'm getting nauseous. "Paula, I'm okay." I squirm to remind her I'm still here.

"Sorry," she says. She stands up, yanking me to my feet in the process. Then she kneels down again to grab the papers that have spilled out of her leather purse.

I stoop to help her collect some pictures that lie scattered beneath a seat. A large black-and-white photo stops me in my tracks. It's of Lars and O'Malley, sitting together at an outdoor café! My mind starts snapping pictures: *Click*—baguette sandwich on the table. *Click*—Lars gesturing to O'Malley. *Click, click, click.*

As I hand the picture back to Paula, I raise an eyebrow at her.

She snatches the photo from me and stuffs it into her bag. "Not here, Edmund." She pulls me by the arm as the train stops and everyone piles out. We hurry over to the stairs and up into the fresh air.

It's still raining. I stand on the sidewalk, arms folded, waiting for an explanation. She ignores me and whips out her cell phone, punching in a number. "It's me," she says after a few seconds. "Just had an accident in the subway. One of those I-beams from the old tracks. Little Red's secure. Yep." She hangs up.

Little Red? Are you kidding me? *That's* my new code name?

"Was that Bovano?" I ask.

She shakes her head. "Chief Williams." We stand there staring at each other, the rain wetting our hair and faces. "You weren't supposed to see that picture," she finally says.

I shoot her a *No duh* look. "Tell me about Lars and O'Malley. I deserve to know."

She shifts her purse from one shoulder to the other. "There's not much to say."

I let out a sound of disbelief and point to her jacket. "You just had your hand on a gun. That's not normal, Paula! Tell me what's going on!"

She runs a hand over her wet hair. "O'Malley vanished a year ago. That picture was taken in England, the week before he disappeared."

"So you guys lied to me. Lars and O'Malley *are* buddies and they're in town with some evil plan."

"No." She shakes her head hard. "We confirmed Lars is in Germany. That's the truth. Oh, thank goodness, a cab!" She waves frantically at a taxi with an in-service light. The car pulls over and we climb in.

We don't speak during the ride home. Her words about Lars bother me. If the cops confirmed Lars is in Germany, then why do I need all this extra security?

When we reach the safety of my apartment building, she walks me to the front entrance, her forehead creased with worry. "Look," she says quietly. "I'd appreciate it if you didn't tell anyone about the picture. I could get fired."

"I won't say anything. For your information, I already suspected that Lars and O'Malley are a team. What else do you know? Tell me. Please."

She's silent a moment. "I can't," she finally says. "Look, Edmund, we need your help. You are brilliant and you see things we don't and you draw perfect pictures. But that's as far as this arrangement goes. My job is to keep you safe. Your job is to draw."

I sigh. "Fine. But I need a favor."

"Oh?" She eyes me warily.

"Can you change my code name? Make it Big Red,

or maybe Hulking Manly Red . . . *anything* but Little Red?"

She laughs and holds out her hand to shake mine. "Deal."

That night I sketch the picture of Lars and O'Malley at the café. Then I study it for more than an hour. At first glance, they seem like two people at a business lunch with sandwiches. But something's off in O'Malley's expression. He looks stressed.

There's a napkin on the table to the left of Lars's hand. It's folded differently than the other napkin, shaped into a lumpy square instead of a smooth triangle. I squint. Is something black hiding beneath the napkin edge? A gun? Has Lars placed a gun on the table? No wonder O'Malley looks worried. Are they friends, or enemies?

And what does that mean for me?

Chapter 6

FRANK'S TANK

11:02 A.M., FRIDAY

The next day in chemistry class, Jonah and I are sitting at our lab table, waiting for Mr. Frank to give us instructions. The chemistry teacher, Mrs. Roberts, had to go on emergency maternity leave, so our sixth grade science teacher, Mr. Patterson (a.k.a. Mr. Pee), was supposed to cover the class. But after the first day, it was clear Bovano knew a lot more about chemistry than Mr. Pee did, so Bovano took over. At first Mr. Pee sat in the back and zoned out, but yesterday he stopped coming altogether.

I slide my art pad over to Jonah and show him the picture of O'Malley and Lars. "I found this," I whisper. "It was taken a year ago. Are they friends or enemies?"

He stares at the picture, his body so still and quiet

that I wonder if he's breathing. "Enemies. But maybe with a common goal, so they're working together?"

Some kids walk by our table. Quickly I grab the art pad and put it on my lap. "I think Lars is forcing O'Malley to do something." I lean closer. "The police showed me a mug shot of O'Malley from the nineties. That's a long time ago. He's old now and I bet he's retired. Did you see how miserable O'Malley looked in the café picture? Maybe Lars is forcing him out of retirement, ordering him to make a bomb and send it to the NYPD."

Jonah scratches his head. "But why? What does the bomb mean?"

I flip through my drawings under my desk, landing on the picture of the bomb. "I still don't know. This afternoon I'm doing surveillance at the Met. Paula won't talk to me, but I'll try to get some answers out of Bovano. If I can't, I need you ready and in position with Operation Hack. Five o'clock sharp."

His eyes grow wide and he salutes me. "I'm on it."

"Class, listen up," says Mr. Frank. His voice is deep and commanding, and everyone jumps to attention. He points to a word that he's written in huge letters on the whiteboard: *GOLD*. A shudder of treasure-hunter excitement ripples through the room. Everyone sits up a little straighter.

He chuckles. "I knew that would get your attention. Gold," he says, strolling the front of the room with his hands tucked behind his back, "is an element. Number seventy-nine on the periodic table, identified by the symbol 'Au.' Reacts with very few other elements. Today we'll be studying the phenomenon known as crazing. Anyone know what that is?" His beady eyes dart around the room. I think he's really enjoying this teacher stuff.

Silence answers. In a different class, somebody might crack a joke about "crazing" having to do with going crazy over gold, but not in Mr. Frank's class. The first day of school he established himself as a no-nonsense kind of teacher when he made three kids jog laps around the gym for speaking without raising their hands.

He pulls out a white cloth bag that makes a heavy metallic clinking sound when it settles on his desk. "Crazing is when cracks appear on a glazed surface. You may have noticed it on your ceramic cups at home. There's a gold-covered monument in Central Park that suffers from this problem. The William

Tecumseh Sherman Monument, to be exact. It was regilded in a layer of gold just last year, but the gold has already begun to crack. We're going to figure out why."

At the words "gold-covered monument in Central Park," Jonah starts to splutter and cough. Like I said, sometimes he has difficulty with surprises.

"Each set of lab partners will have one gold coin for this experiment." Mr. Frank opens the bag and begins to distribute the shiny coins. "You will also be assigned a chemical. Go find it in the case. I expect these coins to be returned to me by the end of class. And no monkey business. Isn't that right, Mr. Christopher?"

All eyes are now on Robin Christopher, our class thug, who grew five inches over the summer and is now even more menacing. Robin's face goes red and blotchy. "Right, sir," he mutters.

The first day that Mr. Frank made the class loudmouths run laps was the first day he caught Robin picking on a fifth-grader in the hallway. Robin had knocked the baseball cap off the kid's head—I know what that feels like. Anyway, Mr. Frank made Robin do laps *and* pushups *and* sit-ups, and we haven't had any trouble with Robin since.

The class springs into action, putting on white lab coats and safety goggles that make us all look like alien bugs. The goggles are a tricky fit over my glasses, but I manage. Mr. Frank swings by the table I share with Jonah and plunks down a gold coin. With a small smirk, he hands me a piece of paper with the word *water* printed on it.

"Place your assigned chemical in the plastic tank in front of you, add the gold coin, and then observe what happens. Twenty minutes of observation should do it. You may speak to each other quietly, but I expect you to be memorizing the periodic table. Our first test is next week. Anyone scoring below a B will jog laps."

The class nods enthusiastically. They love Mr. Frank. He became an instant hero after the Robin Christopher workout session. I guess if he can take bullets in the shoulder while chasing down bad guys, he can handle a pack of seventh-graders.

Across the table, Jonah fills the tank with water, plops the coin in, and leans in right up close. He starts murmuring in what I think is Hebrew, his fingers doing a little *tappity-tap-tap* on the tank. Some water sloshes over the edge. This is Jonah "observing quietly."

Most adults think Jonah is really spazzy (he is) and therefore kind of dumb (he isn't — he's the smartest person I know). He has ADHD, which stands for attention deficit hyperactivity disorder. At times it seems as if he's not paying attention, as if he's too hyper to focus. He explained to me that he has a million things running through his mind all at once, and has a hard time slowing them down. For example, right now he's probably thinking about gold, water, the monument in Central Park, Hebrew school, peanut butter, Greek battle tactics, and *Walter the Flying Cow.*

I sit back and observe. The coin is just sitting in the water, where I suspect it will continue to sit for centuries without any change.

Milton slides his stool over so he's sitting beside me. "We need to talk," he says.

"Not here," Jonah hisses, no longer in his Hebrew-chanting trance.

Milton frowns. "No, I mean, we have to talk about the carnival. I'm in charge of the game booths. You guys haven't signed up yet." He pulls out a clipboard and pen. "Which one do you want to cover?"

The carnival — I forgot! "What is there?" I ask.

"There are two shifts," Milton says. "The one o'clock or the three o'clock. You have to stay at your station for two hours, no excuses." He clears his throat, reading from the clipboard. "First is the maze. Second is the bottle cap toss. Third is the potato sack race . . ." He doesn't pause for a breath. I zone out after number seven. Jonah's not listening either. He's stirring the water in the tank with a pencil, trying to create a whirlpool strong enough to make the coin move upward.

"And we need parents to chaperone the dance," Milton finishes. He wiggles his eyebrows at me from beneath his goggles.

The Carnival Dance is the first dance of the year, and my first dance *ever*. Just thinking about it makes my palms sweat. Some kids go with groups of friends, and some go with dates. According to the Senate rumor mill, Jenny Miller's best friend, Andrea Birman, told Kevin Heckles, who told Alan Stoddard, who told Jonah that Jenny's hoping I ask her to the dance. But what if it's just a stupid rumor? What if I ask her and she turns me down?

"I'll do the ring toss," I say, ignoring his comment about the dance. Jonah lifts his head up. "I'll do the bottle cap thing." He stops stirring the water. "Can we do the one o'clock shift? That way we can hang out after."

Milton nods and jots something down. He sifts through the papers on his clipboard. "We still need a teacher for the dunk tank. Hey, Mr. Frank," he suddenly shouts across the classroom. Is he nuts? Does he not understand the wrath of Detective Frank Bovano?

Bovano lumbers toward us, looking extremely unhappy. But Milton's oblivious. "Sir, would you volunteer to be the teacher in the dunk tank for this year's carnival? It's for a great cause, and it's really an honor to be asked. Only our most favorite teachers are chosen."

Someone at the table next to us says, "That's it—Frank's Tank! Frank's Tank!" More kids join in with a chorus of "Will you do it, Mr. Frank? Will you?"

Bovano stops his approach, blinking at the students as if he's not quite sure whether he's lost control of the classroom. All twenty kids smile back at him, begging him with bright *We love you, pleeeease do it* grins.

For a brief moment, I imagine Detective Bovano

falling into a tank of cold water. The thought fills me with enormous joy.

A muscle twitches under Bovano's left eye. "Sure," he says through gritted teeth. The class erupts into loud applause.

This year may hold some promise after all.

Chapter 7

HACKED

5:13 P.M., SAME DAY

Being inside a police surveillance van is not as cool as you might think. Sure, there are gadgets and switches and blinking lights, but I'm not allowed to touch anything. Plus it's a small cramped space that's growing warmer and smellier by the second.

We're parked on Fifth Avenue across from the Metropolitan Museum of Art, a.k.a. the Met. We're back on Museum Mile, the same place I went undercover as an art student last year. I pretended to study famous works of art while observing the faces around me. But now I have to do my observing stuffed in the back of a white van that has a FRANK'S FLOWERS logo printed on the side.

At least Paula's here. She's sitting between me and Bovano, humming softly to herself. The two of them have a workstation that consists of a small desk, two computers, and three television monitors. I have a seat in the corner with one small TV screen that's linked to a camera inside the Met, and that's it.

Paula flashes me an extra-big smile. She watches me with a curious expression as if I'm a zoo exhibit. I guess she's only seen me in school mode, and now that I'm on the job, she expects something magical and brilliant to happen. I stare at the television screen. I memorize the faces walking by. I blink. Yep, that's about it.

My memory works differently from most people's. I can see all the details of a scene clearly in my mind as if I were staring at a photograph. Combine that with my artistic talent, and it makes me the perfect human camera, able to churn out accurate pictures on command.

"I need to know your head's in the game," Bovano grunts. It takes me a second to realize he's speaking to me.

I look over at him. "Of course," I say. Why wouldn't it be?

He raises a bushy eyebrow. "Just ask her to the dance and get it over with."

"What? How . . . who?" I splutter.

He shakes his head. "You're not the only one who's good at observation. Just do it. Quick and painless, like ripping off a Band-Aid."

Only Jonah knows about my crush on Jenny. It feels as though Bovano's hacked into my brain. I fold my arms and stare at the screen as if to prove that I am fully able to focus on our mission. We will *not* be discussing girls.

After a painful moment of listening to Bovano get his large body comfortable in the small vinyl seat, we get down to business. "I have two faces for you, Eddie," he says. Paula leans out of the way so he can hand me some photographs. "These men are known thieves. Real professionals. Our job is to find them."

I study the mug shots, planning to draw their faces tonight. The first guy I decide to nickname Snaggle because he has really crooked teeth that look like monster fangs. The second guy has the biggest muscles I've ever seen, so I name him Rock. With his bald head and gray clothing, he looks like a human boulder.

"And you think they're planning on stealing something European?" I ask, referring to my monitor's

SNAGGLE AND ROCK

being linked to a camera stationed in the European Sculpture and Decorative Arts section of the Met.

Bovano eyeballs me a moment. "A diamond exhibit is coming to the Met in October," he finally admits. "*Diamonds of Royal Europeans.* There was a recent . . . incident that leads us to believe someone is a little too interested. We think it's those men."

The recent incident he's talking about must be the duchess and her stolen crown. "What have these men stolen before? Jewels? Art?"

He waves me off. "You don't worry about that."

Jonah and I knew this would happen. We knew Bovano wouldn't cooperate, which is why we devised the clever yet highly illegal idea of Operation Hack. But before I go through with it, I try one last time to reason with Bovano. Surely he must trust my skills after how much I helped him last year. Taking a deep breath, I decide to go for it:

"Lars liked European art," I say. "Are these perps connected to Lars? Part of his new gang?" I hold up the two mug shots he gave me.

Bovano doesn't answer. Paula bites her lower lip and examines her fingernails.

"What about O'Malley?" I ask. "Are they connected to him? What if I see O'Malley at the Met? What then?"

Bovano shakes his head. "Patrick O'Malley has nothing to do with this. He works alone. And Lars is out of the country. Forget about him." He jabs a thick finger at my television monitor. "You focus on faces. Got it?"

"Let's talk about the bomb," I go on. "It was flashing the time 24:11, but what time was it delivered? Does the department keep track of that kind of thing?" My mouth is firing questions and I can't stop. "All of these numbers could be important. If O'Malley and Lars—"

"They aren't," he snaps. "Need I remind you what happened the last time you interfered with an investigation? You were almost killed. You are a sketch artist and a camera, not a detective." He points to the monitor again. "Get to work."

The last time I interfered with the investigation, I *solved the crime.* Has he forgotten that detail?

He leaves me no choice.

I pretend to get back to work. After a few minutes, I glance over at Paula and Bovano. They're busy analyzing blueprints of some kind. "Exits should be covered there and there," Bovano mutters to Paula. He gestures to the prints with a pen.

I slide my cell phone from my pocket and fire off a one-word text to Jonah:

Go

Instantly my armpits start to sweat. Jonah's working over at the public library so they can't trace the hack to his house. He's using a fake ID that he bought at a sketchy mini-mart on the corner near his apartment building.

We got the NYPD's server name and general password from Milton. Turns out Milton's mom doesn't have access to all the police reports we need, due to her lower security clearance. Enter Jonah Schwartz. Once he logs onto the NYPD website, he'll have to figure out Bovano's personal password. I suggested Italian foods like "spaghetti" or "lasagna," or even a full sentence like "Children annoy me." When I mentioned that to Jonah, he scolded me for being negative about Bovano, claiming that "he's the coolest teacher ever and a really nice guy." No comment.

One minute and thirty-five seconds later, Jonah texts me back:

I'm in—Psswrd EddieRed!

I almost drop the phone. *I'm* Bovano's password? I don't know whether to be flattered or alarmed. I try to put it out of my mind.

Suddenly Bovano's cell phone rings. His ring tone is Darth Vader's march theme. "Yeah," he answers. "No, I'm in the van. I'm not logged on. What do you mean?" He types something into his computer. "I'm locked out!" He glances over at me. I force my face into a neutral expression.

Turning so I'm hunched over my TV monitor, I fire off another quick text to Jonah:

Abort!

He doesn't respond. I peel my shirt away from my sweaty body. What will Bovano do to us if he finds out? Community service? Jail time? Flunk us in chemistry?

Finally my phone buzzes:

5!

Huh? Five what? Bad guys? Targets? Okay, I know Jonah's in a hurry to read everything before he has to pull the plug, but I need more info. I check on Bovano again. He's busy staring angrily at his computer, so I text Jonah back:

5 what?

A minute passes. Two minutes. "I'm telling you," Bovano snarls at the poor soul on the other end of the line, "I'm not on my account. Someone might be hacking me. Put a trace on. Do it now!" He hangs up and throws the phone onto the desk in front of him. Paula murmurs something. I look over in sympathy. That's what an innocent person would do, right?

Three minutes. Bovano's phone rings again and he answers. "Tell me some good news," he says. "No? Fine. No, I understand. Yeah, I'll change the password." He sighs and hangs up the phone. My breath leaves my lungs in a rush. I cover it with a cough.

I stare at the monitor in front of me, pretending to be engrossed by two women walking by a sculpture. My phone vibrates one more time in my hands. I glance down at Jonah's text:

5 Eddie bombs!!!

Chapter 8

THE FOX

1:13 P.M., SUNDAY

How much information have Bovano and Paula been hiding from me? Two weeks ago *five* fake bombs were found around the city, all with that same creepy message: *1 — Eddie will know what this means.* According to the police reports, they were exactly like the one I saw at the station, with O'Malley's twist of green wires and the gluten-free dough strapped to the digital clock. In addition to the one delivered to the precinct, four others were mysteriously reported at those four landmarks Milton told us about: Cleopatra's Needle, Grant's Tomb, the William Sherman statue, and Penn Station.

After reading the details on Bovano's computer files, Jonah wrote down the time that each bomb was phoned in by an anonymous caller, as well as the time that was flashing on the timer itself. I separated them into two lists:

Day	Time called in	Time on bomb
Bomb 1: Mon	9:24	24:11
Bomb 2: Tues	5:16	16:11
Bomb 3: Wed	3:22	12:82
Bomb 4: Thurs	1:16	2:39
Bomb 5: Fri	9:24	16:11

Bombs one and five were called in at the same time, but on different days. Is that important? Yesterday Jonah slept over and we analyzed and reanalyzed the numbers until our brains were a mushy mess. Do the times represent city blocks? Dates? Both could be possible.

I sit down at a computer cubicle at the Bronx Library Center. Dad started working here part-time a few weeks ago, and I asked if I could tag along during his afternoon shift today. He keeps grinning and winking at me from the checkout desk.

Poor Dad. He's way overqualified for this position, and he's getting paid less than half of what he was paid at his old job. He pretends not to be worried about money, but just this morning I overheard him and Mom talking about "what if" we moved to a smaller apartment in the Bronx. The Bronx! That's a really long subway ride away from Jonah and Senate. Can my parents even afford to let me return to Senate next year? That's the thing about money problems: they don't go away overnight.

Shoving my worries aside, I read my list of clues and decide to search the name Patrick O'Malley in the library's special People Database. There are 1.7 million results: Actors, lawyers, politicians. Apparently it's a very common name. Nothing about bombs or the IRA pops up.

I take off my glasses and rub my eyes. Then I click on the *New York Times* icon and start scrolling the newspaper site, searching for the Duchess of Ireland. There are a few nice articles about her and her charity work and some public events she'll be attending this week, but no mention of the stolen crown. My guess is that she's keeping it from the public. I wonder if she would give me a cash reward if I found it for her.

If Lars is behind this, why would he target her? I decide to search some articles about Lars and his past robberies, looking for a link between him and the duchess. Nothing. I hope Jonah is having better luck. He's over at Milton's house, looking through more police reports. Milton's mom is away on a trip, so we pounced on the opportunity. There has to be more information about those Eddie bombs somewhere.

My phone vibrates. I look at the screen and frown. It's a text sent from the number 000–000–0000:

Looking for stolen treasure?

I leap to my feet and jerk my head around. Someone's watching me. Quickly I scan the room. It's a beautiful September weekend, so there aren't many people inside. There's a girl seated at a table, reading a magazine. She's about my age. Three other kids sit at another computer and giggle quietly together. I squint at their monitor. They're playing the game Fussy Chickens. An elderly man shuffles by, clutching a thick novel. And a plump woman pushes a cart of books, putting them back on the shelves one by one.

I read the text again and write back:

Who are you?

A moment later, my phone buzzes:

A friend. Call me the Fox. You're looking in the wrong place.

Before I can think clearly about what I'm doing, I text a super intelligent reply:

Huh??

The Fox: The map. The answer is on the map. Gold. Stolen treasure.

Me: Gold?

The Fox: Old gold. We'd make a good team. Text me when you figure it out. Nice to meet you, Eddie Red.

I almost drop my phone. This Fox person knows my code name! Collecting myself, I write:

Figure what out?

No answer.

"Ready to go?" Dad's deep voice sounds behind me. This time I *do* drop my phone. It clatters across the desk and almost lands in a trash can.

"Yep." I scramble to grab the phone, then stuff it into my backpack along with my notebook and art pad. I force a smile onto my face and follow Dad out the doors and down the steps, glancing over my shoulder one final time. Is anyone following me? Anyone watching behind those big windows?

I take a deep breath and try to calm down, but the hair on the back of my neck feels electrified. Someone out there knows who I am, knows my cell phone number, knows that the cops call me Eddie Red. Lars . . . It has to be Lars. The cops swear that Lars is in Germany and isn't a threat. But what if they're wrong? I can't take that chance.

There's only one thing left to do.

It's time to go undercover.

Chapter 9

IRISH JIG

4:15 P.M., TUESDAY

"The Fox could be anyone," Jonah says.

"He knew my code name," I reply. "The police are the only ones who call me Eddie Red. Lars had a girlfriend who worked for the police, remember?" Last year the police sent an officer, a woman named Alisha, undercover to infiltrate Lars's gang of thieves. She ended up switching sides and betraying the cops. "I bet she told him all about me. It *has* to be Lars. Who else could it be?"

I lean forward to pay the taxi driver fifteen dollars out of the measly eighty bucks I've earned from the police. Then we slide out of the cab on the corner of Tenth and Fifty-First. It's showtime.

After school we told Paula we were going to play video games until my parents got home (they're both working late tonight, but Paula doesn't need to know that). We promised to lock the door and not open it for any strangers, so she left. When the coast was clear, we jumped in a cab and drove over here.

Our disguises consist of the clothing we wore to school today. Nothing more, nothing less. At first I was nervous about sneaking out, but Jonah assured me that no one ever pays attention to kids on the street. I tested his theory by walking past the cop stationed in an unmarked police car outside my building. The cop didn't even blink.

"If Lars is the one texting you," Jonah says as the cab drives away, "then why would he call himself the Fox?"

"I don't know. To trick me? Make me think he's someone else?" I've researched a ton of news articles about Lars the past two days. No mention of the word *fox,* or any animal for that matter.

We cross the street, heading for a plain cream-colored building with the words IRISH ARTS CENTER written in large green letters. Mom took me here once for a dance performance. There's a special kid art festival today, a festival that the Duchess of Ireland herself is attending. It's perfect.

We stand outside, pretending to examine the art-work in the window. The theme is "Two Worlds, One Ireland." Kids from all over the city painted pictures of both Manhattan and Ireland, sometimes meshing the two landscapes together in a single frame.

The history of the Irish in New York is actually pretty fascinating. They've been very influential in shaping the city. Back in 1845 when the Great Fam-ine hit Ireland, millions of starving people fled their country and came to the United States. By 1850, the Irish made up a quarter of New York's population. Practically everyone I know has a little Irish blood in them. People love to celebrate their Irish heritage, as evidenced by the big turnout for today's event.

I look up and down the street to make sure we're not being followed. Jonah clears his throat. "Here comes a family. Act natural." His leg starts to twitch, which for him *is* acting natural.

I glance over my shoulder in time to see a mom and dad strolling with two kids a little younger than us. We wait until they open the doors, then slide in behind them as if we're a part of their group.

Shuffling past an information desk, we enter a large white room crawling with kids. There's amateur artwork all over the walls, with a few framed paintings by famous Irish artists in the center of the room. I stop in front of a really funky painting by Louis le Brocquy. He's known for doing portraits that capture the person's face beneath the face, making them almost appear skeletal. Totally cool and creepy.

Jonah pulls me away. "She's over there," he whispers, gesturing with his head. The duchess is by the far wall, shaking people's hands in a receiving line. Flanked by two security guards, she's wearing a peach suit and large set of pearls, her brown hair swept high into a regal bun. She's smiling as she talks to a lady and squirming toddler. She seems like a people person, which bodes well for our mission.

Jonah gets in line to meet her while I stroll the room, searching for a guard to speak to. When I asked Jonah why *he* should be the one to meet the duchess, he said, "I have red hair. She'll think I'm one of her people. And you're used to working with cops, so you should be interviewing the guards." I guess he has a point.

Scanning the crowd, I find a guard standing by an emergency exit, his navy blue uniform crisp and sharp. All the guards here must know what happened with the stolen crown on Fifth Avenue. Squaring my shoulders, I pull out a notepad like a kid reporter and stride up to him. "Sir, may I—?"

"No," he says, his face tense and stern. He points over my shoulder. "The exhibit's that way." He opens the emergency door and slides inside, closing it in my face.

These guys are as friendly as Detective Bovano. I look over to see if Jonah's having more luck. He's reached the duchess and is currently doing a little dance for her. An Irish jig?

The duchess laughs as Jonah bows. He starts talking, his hands gesturing wildly the way they do when he gets excited. The smile fades on the duchess's face. She touches her hair as if thinking of the stolen crown. The guards frown and stride forward as if they're going to remove Jonah. Uh-oh, this visit might be a lot shorter than we planned.

I'm not going to get anywhere with these stressed security guards. I need to find someone else knowledgeable about what goes on around here, someone who's the eyes and ears of the IAC. My gaze settles on a short figure pushing a cleaning cart on the other side of the room where the exhibit ends. Bingo.

I pass by a wall covered in landscape paintings of Ireland, glancing at a particularly pretty one with fields of purple and white flowers. *Stay focused,* I scold myself. Slipping between two tall women, I call out to the janitor, "Excuse me, sir?"

He stops and looks at me in confusion. His dark hair is trimmed almost to the scalp, and he has tired brown eyes. I flash him my very best grateful-kid smile as I approach. "Can I ask you a few questions?"

"You should be with your parents." He takes a cloth from his pocket and wipes his brow. "Security's tight. You can't wander past the exhibit."

"I'm doing a special report for my school newspaper," I explain. "You must hear a lot of what goes on here." I'm not just sweet-talking this guy; it's a true fact that janitors have a ton of information. Henry, the janitor who works at my school, knows *everything* that goes on there, from who stuck gum on the ceiling to the name of the delivery guy who stocks the vending machines. I'll bet he even knows Mr. Frank's true identity.

"We heard that the Duchess of Ireland had her crown stolen right on Fifth Avenue," I say. "Does that ring a bell?"

He puts the cloth back in his pocket, his eyes darting nervously around the room. At first I don't think he'll talk, but then he says, "Is this off the record? Because I could get fired."

"I understand," I say. "It will be totally anonymous."

He nods. "Okay, then. Yes, her crown was stolen." He leans in closer. "The thieves left a message when they robbed the truck. 'Tell them the camera is next,' they said." He waves a hand in the air. "We had all the security cameras replaced two months ago. Now everyone's worried that the thieves want to steal them."

The camera? A chill slides down my spine. That's what the police call me. Bovano's always saying, "You are a camera, not a detective."

"Was there anything else unusual?" I ask. "Did they say what the robbers looked like?"

"Very bad teeth." He starts to push his cart. "That's all I know. Better go back to your family."

My family? Oh, right. "Thanks for your time." I smile and quickly locate Jonah. He's being escorted out of the building by two beefy blond men.

I find him out on the sidewalk. The guards are scolding him for upsetting the duchess. He hangs his head like a sorry kid, but when his eyes meet mine, they're alive with excitement. I know that look. He's just figured something out, an important clue.

As soon as the guards leave, we start walking in the direction of a bakery we saw on the way here. Going undercover works up an appetite. Quickly I tell Jonah what the janitor said. "The guy with bad teeth *has* to be the same guy from the mug shot that Bovano showed me," I say. "We have to find him." We cross the street. "What did the duchess say?"

Jonah flips on his sunglasses. "She got really upset when I asked her about the crown. She started muttering, 'The robbers sent a message: *No royal is safe in New York.* She repeated it three times: *No royal is safe in New York.* I felt kind of bad for her."

We hang a right down Tenth Avenue. "The 'royal' comment must refer to the royal jewels exhibit coming to the Met," Jonah continues. "Lars robbed the duchess to get the cops' attention. He *wants* them to know what he's up to. It's much more challenging and fun for him."

"Just like last time," I say, referring to how Lars sent his men to specific meeting places, knowing the police were watching him. He wanted the cops to understand that he was playing a chess game with them, using the city blocks on the map as the game board. I pause to tie my shoe. "What do you think about the 'the camera is next' comment? What if it's me?"

He shrugs. "It's a long shot, but if the robbers know you have a photographic memory, then they might be talking about you. And if that's true, then the police would be nervous for your safety. It explains why you have so much police protection."

That same chill shivers on my skin again. *The camera is next.* Nervously, I look over my shoulder. No one's following us on this sunny day. I decide that it must mean something else, an expensive camera of some kind needed to complete their heist. I refuse to live in fear.

"What's our next move?" Jonah asks. We stop in front of the bakery window. A warm buttery smell drifts in the air and my stomach growls.

"Chocolate-filled croissants. And then—"

A man on the corner of the block catches my eye. He has tan skin and looks like he's from India. I blink. Why does he seem familiar? Quickly I flip through a bunch of pictures in my head. I think I saw him at the Met four days ago, dressed as a museum security guard.

He glances at me over his shoulder and shakes his

head, as if saying no to me. Then he turns the corner and disappears from view.

"Wait!" I call out. I run down the street, Jonah hot on my heels. Rounding the corner, the sunlight momentarily blinds me. I look up the block and down the block.

He's gone.

Chapter 10

HORSE BUTT

―

10:35 A.M., SATURDAY

On Saturday, Paula comes to the school gym with me to paint a horse's butt. The eighth grade made a gigantic Trojan horse out of papier-mâché for Homecoming in a couple of weeks. It's so huge that it's sitting in parts and can only be assembled outside on the day of the parade.

"You okay, Eddie? You seem distracted," Paula says.

I open my mouth, ready to tell her everything: the texts from the Fox, my theory about "the camera" and how it's another message for Eddie Red. But it all sounds so unbelievable: *I'm worried that a famous criminal is stalking me and texting me about gold and stolen treasure and maps.*

"I was just thinking about that Indian guard I saw," I explain. I drew a picture of him yesterday and gave it to her, telling her that I saw him while strolling the street with my father. I said we were out searching for a birthday present for my mom. Obviously a major lie, but I don't think she'll mention it to my parents. She trusts me.

"I'm looking into it, I promise," she says.

I nod and get back to painting. Here's the weird thing: the Indian man kind of, sort of, looks like the Irishman O'Malley. He's a lot younger and has mostly Indian features, but his nose is long and his lower lip is fuller than his upper lip, just like O'Malley. I thought about it all night long. A lot of Indian people live over in Great Britain. What if O'Malley married an Indian woman and they had a son? An O'Malley junior? The guy I saw would be the right age, maybe midtwenties.

At home I stared at the two pictures side by side for hours. Could they be related? It's so hard to say. I think I'm losing my edge. And why was the guy staring at me like he knew me? Why did he shake his head?

Paula brushes a piece of curly hair out of her face and keeps painting. My parents couldn't come out with me today so they called Paula to see if she'd mind being my protection for a few hours. I think

she's really enjoying herself. She keeps laughing with the other kids, teasing them about the big brown lumps that are supposed to be a horse. Why couldn't *she* be the undercover chemistry teacher assigned to my school?

This morning I gave her a thank-you present for being such a good guard. I called it a New York City survival kit, complete with a whistle for hailing cabs, a waterproof street map, an I ♥ NY keychain, and a small umbrella that Mom had from her real estate firm's gift sets. And since Paula must get bored waiting around for me during school, I also included a list of my favorite bagel and deli places, as well as cool parks to check out around the city.

Paula glances up, distracted by something behind me. With a mischievous smile, she moves away toward the horse's stomach. I turn around. Jenny Miller is coming over with a Trojan costume in her hand.

"Hi, Edmund," she says. She's wearing a long patchwork skirt with tiny bells on it that jingle when she walks. She doesn't dress like the other girls in my class, which is one of the reasons I like her. She's not afraid to be different.

"Hi." I stand there like an idiot, the brush in my hand dripping brown paint all over my sneakers.

"I'm working on the costumes and I need to see if this fits you." She unfolds the shirt and holds it up to me. It's a plain brown tunic that we're all wearing under our "armor," which consists of cardboard and duct tape.

Now's my chance. Nine simple words: *Jenny, will you go to the dance with me?* I put my paintbrush down, take the shirt from her, and slide it on. "It fits," I say lamely. I pull the shirt off and fold it back up.

"Good. That was easy." She flips through a few color-coded pages. Pink, yellow, orange, green. I wonder what it all means. Finally she lands on a red page. "I'll file you under red because, you know . . ." She points to my red baseball cap, then writes something down. She clears her throat. "I saw that you're working the first shift at the carnival. I am too. Maybe we could hang out after?"

"Yeah," I say. "Yes. That would be great." I take a deep breath. "Jenny, will you go —"

"Hey, Jenny, Mrs. Smith needs you." Milton's voice is a sledgehammer destroying the moment. Jenny looks at me as if she wants to say something more. Instead she says, "See you later," and quickly walks away. I ignore Milton and start painting the horse butt again, biting the inside of my cheek so I don't say anything I'll regret.

"Sorry," he mutters. "I didn't mean to interrupt. Mrs. Smith was having a cow about the shields. Jenny's the only person who has any idea what's going on." He picks up a paintbrush to join me. "Where's Jonah?"

"At temple." It's probably a good thing Jonah's not here. He and I have been whispering together a lot at school, and people are starting to think we're antisocial.

"I found those names you wanted." Milton hands me a folded piece of paper. Yesterday I told Milton we overheard Bovano talking about some guy named Fox, and asked him to investigate. "Eight people with the last name Fox have been arrested in the past six years," he says. "That's as far as my mom's computer files go. There was one interesting arrest made about a year ago. A woman named Paulette Fox was caught stealing diamond rings from that fancy jewelry store Tiffany's."

A woman named Paulette? That's a strange coincidence. I glance over at Paula, who has stepped away from the horse and is now frowning down at her phone. She looks as upset as she did that day on the subway. How much do we really know about her? The police trust her, but they've trusted other cops who ended up betraying them.

I shove the paper in my pocket and pop open a new container of brown paint. "Thanks," I say to Milton. "I really appreciate it."

"No problem. We make a great team."

I pause. Those are almost the same words that the Fox texted me last week. Is Milton the Fox? I glance at him. He's wearing a red T-shirt with a ketchup bottle on it that reads, *I put ketchup on my ketchup.* There's no way this kid is a mastermind criminal. Right?

"Something's going on," he whispers after a moment.

I stiffen. "Oh?"

He nods, dipping his brush in the paint can and slopping on more brown. He's messing up a patch of my careful brushstrokes. I know it's just a horse butt, but still. An artist must keep high standards.

"It's Bovano's story about the mob laundering money at Senate," he says. "It doesn't add up. First of all, there's no mention of Senate Academy in any of the police reports. Second of all, I've been paying close attention to the kids at school. There's no way the Mafia is involved here." He stops painting and stares at me.

My mouth goes dry. "Is there a third of all?"

"You," he says quietly. "I don't understand you and Bovano. He follows you everywhere. The other kids don't notice, but I do. He tracks you."

I force a shrug. "I've known him forever. He's like an overprotective uncle."

Milton rests his paintbrush on the tray and wipes his hands on a rag. "You missed some," he says, pointing to a spot of white newspaper on the horse. Then he squints at me as if trying to pry into my brain. "You can trust me, you know."

"I know," I say, and I mean it.

But I can't tell him about Eddie Red. I just can't.

Chapter 11

GRANT'S TOMB

2:23 P.M., SUNDAY

"Who is buried in Grant's Tomb?" Dad says. "Now, *that* is an interesting question." He giggles. He's asked me the same question five times since we arrived at the General Grant National Memorial (a.k.a. Grant's Tomb).

"Ha ha, Dad. Very funny."

Apparently there was a famous quiz show that used to ask that question for laughs. The answer is "no one." It's a riddle. General Ulysses Grant and his wife are entombed here, but they aren't buried. Their bodies rest side by side in two stone coffins called sarcophaguses that sit aboveground. Hence, no one is "buried" here. Hilarious, right?

Dad and I just walked out of the dome-shaped memorial and into the warm September air. I look around for any unusual activity, but nothing seems out of place or suspicious. It's hard to believe there was a fake bomb with my name on it delivered here a couple of weeks ago.

We sit down on the stone steps and Dad pulls out a bottle of water. The monument is set in a tree-lined plaza next to the Hudson River, which makes it a very peaceful but windy spot. We used to come here a lot with my Grandma Lucille before she died. She loved Grant, calling him "a hero who freed our people." It feels strange to be here without her. I wonder if Dad feels the same way. She was his mom, after all.

"I've never understood that joke about Grant," an elderly lady says behind us. "Do you work here?" She's speaking to my dad, who is dressed in a navy suit coat and bow tie and looks like he *could* work here as a guide. When I objected to his fashion choice this morning, he said, "You never know when you're going to meet a future employer." I guess I can't blame him for wanting to find a better job.

"Why no, madam," he says, rising to his feet and giving her a quick bow. "But I know a lot about this place. Allow me to explain." He launches into an explanation about the game show and Groucho Marx and other random factoids about how Grant was an important general in the Civil War who eventually became the eighteenth president of the United States. The lady nods and smiles, obviously thrilled.

I ignore them and pull out a map of the city. After analyzing the clues all morning at home, I've decided to take the Fox's advice and look at a map.

I've circled the police station plus the four landmarks where the Eddie bombs were delivered. I told my dad I was doing a project on the effects of weather and acid rain on New York's monuments for chemistry class. He was psyched to take me on a father-son outing. The plan is that I'll hit Grant's Tomb while Jonah covers the Sherman statue in Central Park. We'll visit Penn Station and Cleopatra's Needle next week.

Looking at the map, I don't see how the sites form a pattern. But if Lars is behind the bomb scares, then it all *has* to mean something. Everything he does involves puzzles and games. But what? What do Grant's Tomb and Cleopatra's Needle have in common?

A man walks up the wide staircase, his face turned away. He's thin and wiry and dressed head-to-toe in black. Alarm bells ring in my head. Lars? I can't be sure. He walked by too fast and now he's entering the door of the mausoleum.

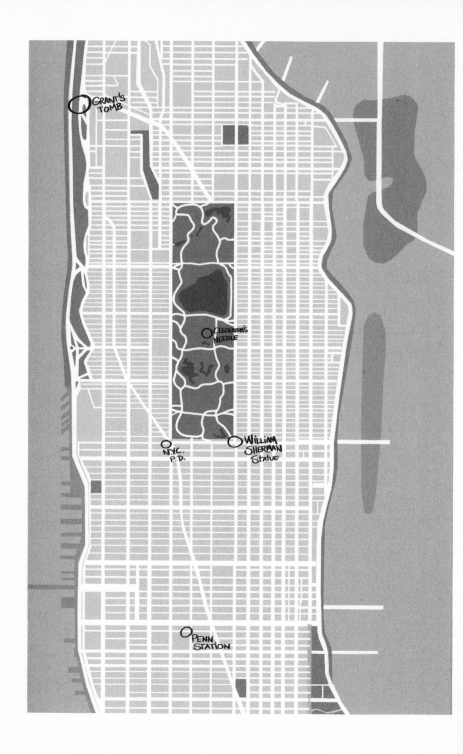

I glance around for my father, who isn't here. He must have gone inside with the woman. Wasn't he supposed to be worried about my safety? Leave it to Dad to forget about me during a history lesson.

Quickly I fold up the map and stand, reaching for the pepper pen in my pocket. I jog up the steps and into the mausoleum. The door creaks open. I squint in the darkness as my eyes adjust to the dim yellow light. My pen is out, safety switch flipped, ready to spray. Dad's not here. I peer over the balcony to the sarcophaguses below on the lower level. He's there with the woman, gesturing to a marble bust.

I hurry toward the staircase. My feet are loud in the quiet chamber. Where's the thin man?

Suddenly someone brushes behind me and I nearly drop the pepper pen. I whirl around. It's him! He's strolling with his hands behind his back, looking at a stained-glass window. I grip my weapon, ready to spray. The man turns his head. Now's the moment, I have a perfect angle . . .

It's not Lars. Not even close.

What am I thinking? I was just about to mace a completely innocent person! I shake my head, disgusted with myself. The police say that Lars is in Germany. I need to trust their information. I stuff the pepper pen back in my pocket and head downstairs for my father. He introduces me to the old lady, who pats my head and offers me a mint.

"Thanks," I say. I pop one in my mouth only to realize it's covered in fuzz. Trying not to gag, I turn away and discreetly spit it into my hand. That's when I see it: a huge map on the wall, tucked behind the stairs. I step closer. It's a map of the Tennessee River and an explanation of Grant's military campaign during the Civil War.

Something tickles at my brain. A clue I might have missed. I've been analyzing the streets and landmarks of New York over and over. When the Fox said that the answer was on the map, I assumed he meant one of New York City. But now a crazy thought occurs to me:

Have I been looking at the wrong map?

Chapter 12

ELEMENTAL, MY DEAR WATSON

8:05 A.M., MONDAY

I wake up in a bad mood. Maybe because it's Monday, or maybe because I barely slept last night, or maybe because my brain's about to explode from the stress of bomb scares and missing crowns and subway accidents and school dances and possibly having to move because we can't afford our apartment. I want to be in bed watching a movie, but instead I'm with Paula walking toward Senate Academy. Detective Bovano looms like a gargoyle at the top of the steps, opening the front door for students.

"Frank will be escorting you to the Met after school," Paula says, gesturing to Bovano with her head. "Don't leave school by yourself. I'll meet you over there."

I nod. Maybe there's a map at the Met I should be looking at. I'll check it out today when I'm there.

I say goodbye to Paula and walk across the short lawn of the school. A group of fifth-graders is laughing and tossing a baseball around. Slowly I trudge up the concrete steps. Mr. Frank opens the door. "We need to talk," he mutters under his breath. "Be in my classroom in two minutes."

Without a word, I turn right and head for the chemistry room.

If I work for the police, how come it feels like *I'm* the one in prison?

By chemistry class, I still haven't spoken with Bovano. This morning he got tangled up in some problem involving kids, a baseball, and a pile of dog poop, so we never had our meeting.

"Time," Jonah says.

I stick a long thermometer into a beaker of ice water that's warming up over a Bunsen burner. Today's experiment: water freezes at 32 degrees and boils at 212 degrees. How long will it take to go from 32 to 212? We have to take a temperature reading every sixty seconds. It's fairly mind-numbing.

"Thirty-five degrees," I say. He writes it down.

Around us, the class is buzzing. Mr. Frank promised us a pizza party if we all got an A minus or higher on last week's test. Everyone aced it, even Jimmy Watson, who's a big blockhead. So today for lunch we're eating pizza from Mario's Pizzeria. I wonder if Bovano is paying or if this little party is courtesy of the NYPD.

Jonah looks around to make sure no one's listening. "What did you find? Any connections with the monuments?"

I shake my head. "No. You?"

"Not really. Time."

"Thirty-six."

He writes it down. "You know that gold statue of William Sherman that Bovano . . . er, Mr. Frank was talking about? The same statue that had the bomb scare?" When I nod he says, "Turns out Sherman was a famous general. He was the one who said, 'War is Hell.' How did I not know about this guy? He's *awesome!* I visited the site three times this weekend. I even left part of a peanut-butter sandwich by his feet. You know, as a kind of offering. Time."

I read the thermometer again. Mr. Frank passes behind us.

"Elements," Mr. Frank suddenly announces to no one in particular. "The most basic substances on Earth. Everything you see around you can be broken down into components read on the periodic table." He stops by Jenny Miller. "Even you, Miss Miller, are nothing more than hydrogen, oxygen, carbon, and some others. The first person to tell me the exact percentages of elements in the human body will get an extra slice of pizza today. But no researching until your experiments are done and wyour lab reports are passed in."

Everyone gets quiet, their faces focused as they race to finish the experiment and claim the pizza prize. You have to hand it to Bovano: he understands that kids will do anything for double cheese, double sauce.

Jonah's staring off into space as if his brain's calculating a million things at once. Which it probably is.

"Time, Jonah," I hiss.

He looks at his watch. "Oh, whoops. Time in three, two, one . . ."

I take another reading. "Forty-four."

He writes the number down and then leans closer. "The Sherman statue is covered in gold. That's an element. What are the others made out of?"

I get where he's going with this. I flip through my mental notes on the monuments, paragraph after paragraph of Internet research scrolling by in my memory. "According to *Wikipedia,* Grant's Tomb is red granite—at least the coffins are. I think there's some bronze decoration as well. And Cleopatra's Needle is made from red granite."

Jonah's leg twitches beneath the lab table. Despite the sturdiness of our workstation, his spazzy movements are strong enough to rattle the jar of ice water on the burner. I try to steady the glass without burning myself. Some of the ice breaks apart with a clink.

"What if the bomb sites represent hidden messages through the periodic table?" he says. "William Sherman is covered in gold. The symbol for gold is 'Au.'" He starts to scribble down ideas in his notebook. "And bronze is made out of copper and tin. Their symbols are 'Cu' and 'Sn.'" He flips the page around to show me:

William Sherman — gold = Au
Grant's Tomb — bronze: copper = Cu, tin = Sn

"I wonder if they might spell a word?" he contin-
ues. "If we put the letters all together. Aucusn . . .
Cusnau . . . Snaucu? I'm going to snack on you?
Maybe it's German."

"Maybe," I say. But I'm pretty sure the answer
doesn't come from a periodic table. I can't get the idea
of a map out of my head. What did the Fox mean
about old gold and stolen treasure? Do the monuments form a secret treasure map? We need a key,
something to unlock their meaning.

I stare at my watch, waiting for sixty seconds to
tick by. Jonah's typing on his computer (hidden beneath the table on his lap) and muttering under his
breath about red granite. He's completely derailed
from the experiment, and I for one do not want to
repeat it after school.

A horrible burnt smell fills my nose. I look down
at our burner, but it seems normal. A few kids make
gagging noises and I turn around to see what's going
on. Jimmy Watson is holding his pencil over the fire,
trying to get the wood to catch. Then he waves his

thermometer near the flame. "How hot do you think fire is?" he says.

Robin Christopher laughs an obnoxious laugh. The two of them are lab partners and are perfect for each other. Big, menacing, and as smart as rocks.

"I dare you," Robin says. I watch in horror as Jimmy moves the tip of the thermometer closer to the flame.

Jonah's eyes go wide under his safety goggles. "They can't possibly be that stupid," he whispers to me.

"Do it!" Robin pushes Jimmy's hand.

"No, don't!" Bovano shouts from three desks over. He lunges for them, but it's too late. The thermometer goes into the fire and explodes, spraying glass and mercury all over. Tiny droplets of silver speckle the lab coats of Jimmy, Robin, and Bovano. These thermometers are supposed to be shatterproof, but are clearly not idiot-proof.

The entire class freezes, everyone holding their breath as if a bomb is about to go off.

"Don't anybody move." Mr. Frank's voice is eerily quiet. Yesterday he told us that mercury is a liquid metal that's extremely poisonous and has been known to turn people insane.

I don't think we'll be having that pizza party today.

Chapter 13

JUNIOR

———

3:22 P.M., SAME DAY

After school, Bovano drives me to the Met. His hair is wild and fluffy from an afternoon spent decontaminating the classroom of mercury. He shifts in his seat and clears his throat, and I can sense that we're about to have our "little chat."

When we stop at a traffic light, he holds up a picture from the front seat. It's the picture I drew of the Indian guy. "Why'd you give this to Paula?" he asks.

Because I knew you'd blow me off? "I thought she could work on it today while you and I were at school," I lie.

"I'm your contact, not her. This is our case. She's a Fed and—" He catches himself before he tells me more. "From now on, all casework goes through me."

A Fed? Jonah's suspicions were correct: Paula works for the FBI. I wonder why she was brought in. The

FBI works on really important national cases. Surely my safety is not the only reason she's been assigned to the job.

And did Bovano just say *our* case? As in, his case and my case? We're a team now?

"I didn't really think it was important," I say, trying to smooth over the situation. "Did you find out the guy's name? He works at the Met, right?"

"Wrong. He was dressed as a guard, but there's no record of his employment there."

"So that's a huge lead, right?" I sit up straighter in my seat.

He shrugs. "Maybe, maybe not."

I stifle a growl of frustration. So much for working as a team. We drive in silence the rest of the way.

Finally we park in the alley beside the Met. Bovano turns off the engine. "We're going inside today," he says, his hands still on the steering wheel. "To the basement storage area. You won't be out in public, so technically we aren't violating your mom's request."

I roll my eyes. If there's one thing that Detective Bovano cares about, it's my mother's opinion.

We exit the car and pass through the service entrance of the museum, then head down a flight of stairs. Bovano flashes a pass card over an electronic pad, which unlocks a door with a loud clank. As I walk behind him, I mull over the new information. The Indian man was dressed as a guard but doesn't work here. Clearly he's been casing the museum. But for what? The diamond exhibit? And of course, the number one question that's always on my mind: Does he have anything to do with Patrick O'Malley or Lars Heinrich?

We head down another flight of stairs and reach a metal door marked RESTRICTED. Bovano pounds on the door so loudly that the echo sounds like thunder around us. After about twenty seconds, an elderly man tugs the door open. He's rail-thin with white hair and a plaid bow tie. His nametag reads KURT TERPE, CURATOR.

"The K-9 unit was just here!" the man says in a high-pitched voice. He motions us through the door with an impatient wave of his gnarled hand. "Dogs! In my museum!" Every sentence comes out in a breathy exclamation. He focuses all his attention on Bovano. If he thinks it's strange that there's a kid tagging along, he doesn't comment.

"I don't know what you expect to find!" he squeaks on. "Everything is intact!"

"This is routine, sir," Bovano explains politely.

"We'll be in and out in twenty minutes." Then he turns to me. "Go find Paula." He points across the vast storage room that's loaded floor to ceiling with statues and framed art, some of it wrapped in sheets, others sitting behind glass cases.

I spot Paula sifting through some papers with gloved fingers. I trot over, narrowly avoiding walking into a huge marble statue of a lady in a toga. "What's going on?" I say.

She shakes her head. "I'm not sure, actually. The Indian man you saw on the street doesn't work here. But he walked around the museum for a solid week, dressed as a guard. As far as we can tell, he never spoke to anyone else, never touched anything. He just . . . strolled."

"Hmm." I rub my chin and look around the basement. It almost feels haunted, with the shadows and the tall shapes draped in cloth. "I'll need to see all of the security tapes."

Paula tilts her head and raises her eyebrows at me.

"What?" Suddenly paranoid, I look down at my shirt to check for any stains. Today was burrito day at school—which I had to eat because the pizza party was canceled—and the salsa got out of control.

She grins. "Okay, Frank Junior. You sounded like him just now. He's beginning to rub off on you."

I narrow my eyes and her smile falters. "Sorry," she mutters. "I'm just nervous. I don't like the feel of it down here. Too cold." She pulls her sweater around her shoulders a little tighter.

Something's going on. Yes, she's joking around, but she's twitchy, her foot tapping as she fiddles with the corner of a manila folder.

"What am I doing here?" I ask.

She shrugs. "Just looking, I guess. Cataloging it in your brain. We need you to see the room how it is now, so when you see the security tapes, you'll notice any differences. A painting out of place, something like that. In case the perp snuck in here without the cameras catching him."

I glance around. There are no maps anywhere that I can see. No jewelry storage, either. The mystery of the stolen crown still bothers me. If Lars was behind the heist, why would he steal it? And what did the thief's message mean about the camera being next? There are no expensive cameras down here, *nothing* that's connected with that robbery.

The section we're standing in houses mostly paintings, and that's what Lars loves best. Paintings by the famous artist Pablo Picasso, specifically. Bovano is still on the other side of the room, so I decide to press Paula for more information. "Are there Picassos in storage?"

She hands me the thick stack of papers she's been sifting through. "I spotted four on the list," she says. "See for yourself. But first—" She hands me a pair of latex gloves.

I snap on the gloves and study the pages. Even with my photographic memory, this will take hours to go through. I wonder if they'll let me make a photocopy.

The heavy metal door slams shut as the curator leaves, and Paula jumps. Very unusual for my calm-and-collected bodyguard.

"Paula," I say in an innocent-kid voice. "Why were the dogs here? Were they sniffing for drugs? Or"—I turn a page of the catalog—"was it for bombs?" My eyes flicker over and meet hers.

She opens her mouth, then closes it. "It's classified," she whispers.

I can't take not knowing what's going on anymore. It's not Paula's fault that I have no information to work with. There's only one person to blame for that.

I march over to Detective Bovano and hand him

the storage catalog. "I'll need a photocopy of these," I announce. He blinks at me, obviously startled by my demand. I go for it. "You want me to report all of my findings to you," I say, "but you won't tell me what's going on. How am I supposed to trust you when you don't trust me? How can we catch the thieves if you refuse to let me help? You said this was *our* case. You owe me this, Detective," I add in a moment of either bravery or stupidity. "Tell me what the dogs were looking for."

He frowns, his bushy eyebrows practically covering his eyes. I fold my arms and stick out my chin. I'm not going anywhere until he answers.

He sighs. "I'll answer *one* question," he finally says. "They were sniffing for bombs."

I open my mouth to ask why, but he holds up a hand to cut me off. "The man dressed as a museum guard was wearing a nametag. Impossible to read with the naked eye, so we zoomed in on it." He pauses and runs a hand through his unruly hair.

"His last name is O'Malley."

Chapter 14

WHAT DID THE FOX SAY?

ALMOST MIDNIGHT, TUESDAY

I can't sleep. I should be worrying about bombs and O'Malley, but all day I've been obsessed with figuring out what the Fox meant about the map. The four landmarks represent clues, I just know it. Earlier today I dragged Jonah to Penn Station *and* Grant's Tomb because I wanted to show him that Civil War battle map on the wall. I've become quite the expert at sneaking past the unmarked police car parked by my apartment. I don't think that guy's doing a very good job, but I'm not about to complain.

Staring up at the glow-in-the-dark stars on my ceiling, I think about what Jonah said in chemistry class, about how the William Sherman statue is gold and that gold must mean something. What do the other landmarks mean? What do they represent? Cleopatra's Needle is Egyptian. Grant is an icon from the Civil War.

I flip on the light and boot up my computer. I input the words *Civil War gold Egypt* into Google. A lot of entries come up about civil unrest in Egypt, including protests and bombings. Down at the bottom of the screen, there's a "related searches" tab and the words *Hidden Civil War gold*.

My pulse quickens. I click on the link and a ton of hits pop up: buried Confederate gold, Civil War hidden treasure, missing Yankee cash, and lost gold on a train.

Lost gold on a train. A creepy feeling curls around my neck. "Penn Station," I whisper.

"Well?" Jonah says. "We're alone. Can you tell me now?"

I've been dying to tell Jonah my new theory all day, but we had to wait until after school because we had stupid "Senate standard testing" in every class.

I look around the quiet plaza. We're sitting on a

South Carolina

RIVERS BRIDGE
STATE PARK

Ⓐ RIVERS BRIDGE STATE
HISTORICAL SITE

State Rd S-5-31

Threemile Branch

Big Branch

State Rd S-5-8

Shalkehatchie River

CONFEDERATE HWY

park bench, surrounded by beautiful autumn leaves in Central Park. Cleopatra's obelisk towers above us. There are cool Egyptian hieroglyphics running up each side, although they're hard to see because of all the weather damage.

"I found something." I pull out the map I sketched last night. "A link between the monuments. I think the person who left the bombs is showing us a treasure map using the New York City landmarks as a key. Check it out."

"South Carolina?" Jonah says.

I nod. "South Carolina during the Civil War."

He stares at me, his forehead wrinkling. "You're going to have to explain."

"Okay. We have four landmarks that had the fake bombs, right? Grant's Tomb, the William Sherman statue, Penn Station, and Cleopatra's Needle." I motion to the enormous obelisk in front of us. "What if they all *represent* something? Cleopatra's Needle is old. Like, three thousand years old. Penn Station represents a train. Grant stands for the Civil War since he was a major hero during that time, and Sherman's statue is covered in gold. Sherman also fought in the Civil War, so that's an added bonus of meaning."

1—Cleopatra = old
2—Penn Station = train
3—Grant = Civil War
4—Sherman = gold (and Civil War!)

"What about the police station?" he says. "A bomb was delivered there, too."

"That was just to get our attention. It's exactly the kind of game Lars loves to play. He *wants* to be noticed. He made direct contact with the police, and *then* he showed them the game. It's just like last time with the chess moves!"

Jonah doesn't speak, just frowns at the list of clues I've made. I continue. "Taken together, the symbols could mean Civil War gold on a train. *Old* Civil War gold."

I point to my map. "Last night I Googled those clues and found an old map of a Civil War battlefield in South Carolina. Get this—a hundred and fifty years ago, a train carrying Confederate gold derailed into a swamp, right near the battlefield. They never recovered the treasure. I found it! Old gold on a map, just like the Fox said!"

Jonah sighs, as if my investigation is what's derailed. Or maybe he's tired of hearing about the Fox. "If Lars is the Fox," he says, "then it might be a trap. Maybe he's deliberately distracting you so you'll look the other way while he robs the Met. Or blows it up."

"If Lars is the Fox," I shoot back, "then he might be tricking the police into watching the Met while he steals Civil War gold."

Jonah's nostrils flare and his cheeks turn red. "You think Lars is going to search a swamp in South Carolina? Seriously?"

"Yes. No. I don't know." I take back my map and cross my arms. Jonah's right. Lars isn't going to muck around in swamps.

"I think you should tell Bovano about the Fox," Jonah adds quietly.

"I will," I say. "But not yet. I need to figure this out. Once the cops know about it, they'll take over and keep me in the dark as usual. The Fox texted *my* phone. My phone, my life."

He stares at me with big blue eyes. "I know," he says. "That's what worries me."

• • •

That night I dream about maps. Old treasure maps,

yellow and wrinkled. Modern city maps with their crisscrossing lines and subway tunnels. I even dream that Bovano's chasing me in the chemistry classroom with a map. Somewhere around two a.m. I wake up in a cold sweat, wondering if I need to go see a therapist.

Images flood my mind. Trains, old gold, Grant and the Civil War . . . *What's your game, Lars? What are you trying to tell me?*

I turn on my computer and start to search. This time, I add one more clue: the name Fox.

The answer leaps off the screen and practically smacks me in the face. Alexander Fox, a treasure hunter from the 1950s. Jewels. Ancient treasure. And gold . . . lost Civil War gold recovered by Fox in 1958. All of which will be displayed at the Smithsonian Museum in Washington, D.C., on October 28. Just a month away!

"Oh!" I slap a hand over my mouth to muffle my slightly crazed laughter. I did it. I beat the Fox!

I pick up my cell to call Jonah, but pause before dialing. There's no way to get in touch with him at this hour. He's not allowed to keep his cell phone in his room after an incident involving a three-hour

phone call to a guy in Taiwan and an online game of
Demons and Warlocks.

Should I take Jonah's advice and tell the police
about this? Or do I text the Fox—who might possibly be Lars—and lure him to a meeting spot where
the police can grab him? Lars is a wanted criminal in
at least five countries. If I help catch him, I bet there
will be a huge cash reward, enough to pay for Senate until I graduate. Last I checked, I've made just
two hundred bucks from this case. It's time to up my
game.

With slightly shaking fingers, I unlock my phone
and text the Fox:

I figured it out.

The screen sits empty. He's probably asleep. Suddenly the phone buzzes. His reply is one word:

And?

I take a deep breath:

**The Alexander Fox treasure exhibit at the
Smithsonian.**

I leave it at that. Again the screen is blank. Maybe I'm nuts. Maybe my theory is totally out there. Then he writes:

Good boy.

My breath leaves me in a rush. I was right. But before I can respond, he sends me another message:

You passed the test.

Test? What test? Whatever — it's time to hook him in. I type:

This is very interesting to me. We should meet up and discuss further.

The phone sits quietly for more than a minute. Finally it vibrates:

We will. Soon.

Now I'm confused. And flustered. He was supposed to agree to meet me at a specific place and time, and then I'd tell Bovano, and then we'd catch him. I write back:

When?

There's a pause, and then:

Soon.

Chapter 15

SWEET POTATO PIE

4:42 P.M., FRIDAY

More bizarre things happen. Yesterday in the surveillance van, Bovano had me watch some security tapes from the Met, footage of the Indian guy O'Malley posing as a museum guard. He stopped and stared at the camera as if he wanted to be seen. And he spent a lot of time looking at Picassos. Does that mean he's working with Lars? I shared my theory with Bovano but he dismissed it immediately, telling me to "focus on the concrete facts."

I also noticed that O'Malley kept returning to the same painting in the Renaissance section, a small portrait of a man with wings. I couldn't see it clearly on the video footage, so I asked Bovano to take me inside the Met to check it out (with my mother's permission, of course). It was a painting of the Angel of Death, smiling and holding a human skull. The Angel of Death!

"But . . . what . . ." I started to splutter. Bovano dragged me away, saying, "Don't get jittery on me. You're safe. I need you to focus."

I almost told him about the Fox right then and there. Almost. I'm still deciding what to do. I showed Jonah the texts about the upcoming treasure exhibit at the Smithsonian. He was shocked and agreed we'd come up with a plan when he sleeps over after the school carnival tomorrow.

Today is Friday and I should be glad it's the weekend, but when I get home from school, even *more* bad news is waiting for me. Mom is in the dining room, pulling out china plates and a lace tablecloth, setting up the table as if the Queen of England is coming for a visit.

"We're having company?" I ask.

"Yes. Can you reach those crystal glasses for me? Second shelf." She gestures to the hutch.

Carefully I pull them down a glass at a time. They're tapered crystal goblets that my parents got on their honeymoon in Prague. Jonah broke one when we were in fifth grade, and I thought my mom was going to have a heart attack. "Who's coming?"

She doesn't answer, just slides into the kitchen, where her famous lasagna and garlic bread are baking. I narrow my eyes. She's ignoring my question, which means she knows I'm not going to be happy with the answer. Lasagna and garlic bread . . . it doesn't take a genius detective to figure out who our mystery guest is.

I push open the kitchen door. "Why?" I demand.

She doesn't look up, just continues to pull salad ingredients out of the refrigerator. "Frank and Paula have done a lot for our family these past weeks. I thought I'd thank them with a nice meal. They live on hot dogs and cereal bars in that surveillance van, you know."

I lean against the counter, letting her words sink in. Detective Bovano and I have been getting along on the job, and I like his chemistry class, I really do. But I see him about ten hours a day. I need a break.

The door buzzer sounds. "That's them," she says.

"What, now? But it's so early!" I need time to prepare for this mentally.

"I'll get it," Dad calls from the living room. I head

out to join him. Might as well get this awkward greeting part over with.

Bovano is in khaki pants and a blue knit sweater, and Paula is wearing a black pantsuit, with her hair pinned up in a bun. She's holding a pie plate. "Sweet potato pie," she says, lifting it up for me to see. "It's my specialty."

She gives me a quick hug before handing me the pie. Then my father hugs *both* of them. I shuffle back a step. There is no way I am hugging Detective Bovano. He's obviously not thrilled with the idea either. He gives me a simple nod, then beelines to the other side of the room, where my father's Revolutionary War artifact collection rests on the hutch. He and Dad discuss the Battle of Trenton for the next twenty minutes while our cat, Sadie—who hates *everyone*—rubs against Bovano's legs and purrs.

Dinner is surprisingly fun. Bovano and Paula entertain us with police stories, including one about the time Bovano went undercover as a woman to infiltrate a group of bank tellers who were embezzling funds. He tripped in his high heels and sprained his ankle the first day. Paula tells us about the first arrest she ever made. She was so excited that she handcuffed the guy to her belt by accident. We laugh all through the meal. But then the pie is served and suddenly all eyes are on me.

"I can escort you to the dance tomorrow," Paula mentions casually as she adds a dollop of whipped cream to my pie (which looks über-delicious, but suddenly I lose my appetite). "I have the night off, and I don't know anyone in town. I might as well be your date." She winks.

Dad's grin is as wide as the Brooklyn Bridge. "Edmund's first dance. I wanted to chaperone but he won't let me."

I take a bite of dessert. "This pie is really good," I say to Paula, desperate to change the subject. "What's in it besides sweet potatoes?"

"I start with a cup of sugar and a stick of—"

"So, did you ask the girl?" Bovano interrupts. He's leaning on his elbows with an alarming lack of table manners, his dark gaze examining me.

"There's a girl?" Mom's eyes go wide. She reaches for her crystal water glass and almost knocks it over. "What girl?"

You know in the cartoons when a character cuts a hole in the floor around the chair of another character, causing him to fall through? I would like that to happen to me right now.

"No one," I say quickly. "It's our little joke from chemistry class."

Bovano's phone rings. "Sorry," he mutters. "I've been expecting this." He gets up and leaves the table.

"As I was saying, I start with a stick of butter and a cup of sugar," Paula says in her soft southern accent. She winks at me again. She and Dad begin to discuss the ins and outs of the high-cholesterol content of southern cooking while I stare at my half-eaten piece of pie.

Bovano returns a minute later. "Great news, everyone." He sits down in his chair with a plop and digs into more dessert. "There was an explosion in an abandoned factory in Germany. Two bodies were found, and one is believed to be Lars Heinrich. They won't know for sure until they run some tests, but they're about ninety-nine percent positive it's him. So this" — he waves a fork at me — "bodyguard arrangement can come to an end. Probably by next week."

All of the adults start chatting excitedly about what great news this is. Bovano points to my pie and says, "Are you going to finish that?" I push the plate toward him and pretend that it's not really weird that he's eating my leftovers like my dad does.

I try to smile and join in the conversation, but I can't escape the doubts nagging at my brain. Lars is brilliant and meticulous when planning his crimes. He's the ultimate control freak. I just can't picture him being so careless as to die in an explosion. Plus, he isn't in Germany; he's in New York. It might be all in my imagination, but I swear I see him everywhere: walking on the street, slipping around the corner, hopping off the city bus. Not to mention that he's texting me under the code name Fox. But I can't tell them that. What would I say? *Hey, guys, I've been text buddies with Lars for two weeks now. I kept that information from you because I want to catch him myself so I can prove my skills and land a full-time job on the force . . .*

Somehow I don't think that would go over very well.

Chapter 16

CODE CRUNCHING

8:35 A.M., SATURDAY

The next morning I wake up with a cold. Detective Bovano had one a few days ago. Not only are we sharing pie and awkward conversation, but we're sharing germs. And to make matters worse, today is the school carnival and I still haven't asked Jenny Miller to the dance.

I sneeze and turn the page of my math book. Jonah backs his chair up, nervously eyeballing me in my germy state. He came over early this morning to help me with math since I'm way behind in class from all our investigating. Our textbooks and papers are spread out all over the kitchen table.

"More cereal, boys?" Mom asks as she bustles around the kitchen, scrubbing the countertop like a madwoman. She has to go downtown to show two apartments, then come back here so we can go to the carnival just after lunch.

"I'll get it," I say, grabbing the box from the counter. I sneeze and reach for a tissue as I sit back down.

She puts a hand on my forehead. Usually I don't like it when she does that, but her hand feels nice and cool on my skin. She frowns, as if her palm senses Major Illness. "You sure you want to go today?"

Gently I shake her off. "I'm fine. I *have* to go, Mom. I'm on student council."

"All right." She pats my shoulder. "I'll get some of Madame Ling's wonton soup for you, no wonton. Sweet and sour chicken for you?" she asks Jonah. When he nods, she smiles. "See you at twelve. Behave yourselves." She grabs her keys from the table and leaves.

"Thanks," we call after her. Madame Ling is a Chinese lady who married a French man, hence her unusual restaurant name. She thinks it's hilarious that I always order a bowl of wonton soup without the wonton, claiming I'm the only person she knows in all of New York City who likes it that way. I love the broth, but the wonton freaks me out. Something about the slimy noodle with a lump of meat in it reminds me of a tadpole.

Jonah taps his pencil on the math book. "Where do you want to start? Matrices?"

"Sure." This week we're doing matrices, systems of numbers arranged in brackets. It's tricky. I stare down at the rows and columns of numbers. They make me think of the bombs and the times they were called in. I pull out the list to take another look:

Day	Time called in	Time on bomb
Bomb 1: Mon	9:24	24:11
Bomb 2: Tues	5:16	16:11
Bomb 3: Wed	3:22	12:82
Bomb 4: Thurs	1:16	2:39
Bomb 5: Fri	9:24	16:11

Jonah taps again on the textbook. "The chapter test is Tuesday, remember? You need to focus."

A hissing sound startles us both. Sadie jumps onto the table, knocking over the box of cereal. She hisses again in case we didn't hear her the first time. I don't know how she got into the kitchen, but I swear that cat is opening doors.

"Thanks a lot, Sadie," I say in disgust, looking at the cereal flakes spilled all over my notebook. I scoop her up carefully so she can't claw me, and put her out in the hallway. She arches her back until the fur sticks out in angry, electrified spikes.

When I return to the kitchen with the door firmly closed behind me, I find Jonah holding the box of Oat Crunchies. He looks like he's seen a ghost.

"Look." He points to the back of the box. It's covered with cartoon kids and the words *Be a Code Cruncher.* There's a letter and number key to help you decode a secret sentence, which is probably an advertisement to buy Cinnamon Oat Crunchies.

I stand there, staring at the numbers and letters. I know we're both thinking the same thing: What if the numbers on the bombs are a code of some kind? Maybe Jonah was on the right track with his chemistry symbols. Maybe someone's trying to send us a coded message!

We sit down and shove our cereal-covered math books to the side. "There are so many types of codes out there," Jonah says. "I wonder . . ." He pulls out his laptop and starts typing.

I look at the list of bombs and their times and decide to test out the numbers by using the code from the cereal box. I come up with XLYXTOMFRTHED-ABDYX. I can kind of pick out some words. TOM FRTHED . . . A guy named Tom? Tom the farthead? I don't share my findings.

Jonah scratches his head. "There's Morse code and scrambled-letter codes. Oh, and the ROT1 code. Remember that from second grade?"

I smile. "Yeah." ROT1 means "rotate one letter forward through the alphabet," so *A* is replaced with *B*, *B* with *C*, and so on. If *A* = *B*, then the word *Dad* would be *Ebe*. Jonah and I used to use this code when we passed notes, but then he made the whole thing so complicated that I didn't know *what* he was talking about.

He's squinting at his screen and mumbling to himself. I stand up and peer over his shoulder. "What about that one?" I say. I point to the words *Caesar shift cipher*. It's more advanced than the ROT1 code. You need a key—for example, *A* = *M*—and then all the letters shift accordingly. If the times on the bombs are truly a code, then we need a key. A key with numbers and letters.

Jonah's still muttering, his fingers flying over the computer keys. I pace the kitchen and stare at the

blue and white tiles beneath my feet. A key . . . a key
. . . I think of the note that was sent with the bombs:
1—Eddie will know what this means. I've never understood why there was a one by my name. Does 1 =
E? Is it that simple?

I sit down and write it out:

1—Eddie will know what this means
1— E

"Jonah," I say. I show him my notes.

His face breaks into a huge grin. "Yes," he says.
"Yes! If *E* equals 1, then *F* equals 2 . . . Yes!"

We both jot the code down in our notebooks. I
assign each letter a number: *E* = 1, *F* = 2, *G* = 3, until
I reach *Z* = 22, then loop back to the beginning: *A* =
23, *B* = 24, *C* = 25, *D* = 26. Now every letter has a
number.

With a burst of adrenaline, I start to scribble out
possibilities. The first times on our list are 9:24 and
24:11. I come up with MFH FHEE. Nope. I try
every possible combination of numbers, all the way
down the list. I blow out a frustrated breath. "Any
luck?"

He shakes his head. "Let's switch the order. Put

the time on the bomb first and *then* the time it was called in."

"Okay." I write *24:11* and *9:24* for the first bomb. *24 11 9 24 . . .*

24 = B
11 = O
9 = M
24 = B

The room is dead silent. I know Jonah's just discovered the same thing I did, because his eyes are blinking fast. I move to the next pair of numbers, reversing their order as well: 16:11, 5:16.

16 = T
11 = O
5 = I
16 = T

"Toit?" I say. That doesn't make any sense.

Jonah's gone pale and is shaking his head. "Test," he whispers. "If you divide the numbers up as sixteen, one, fifteen, and sixteen, you get the word 'test.'" He turns his page so I can see:

$$16 = T$$
$$1 = E$$
$$15 = S$$
$$16 = T$$

Now it's my turn to blink fast. The Fox talked about a test, a test that I passed. What could this all mean? We work and work, decoding the numbers in different combinations, but always with the time on the bomb first, followed by the time it was called in. Just when I feel as if my brain is about to explode, we come up with the following:

BOMBTESTPLAZAMETTOMB

Quickly I separate the letters into five words:

BOMB TEST PLAZA MET TOMB

"It looks like a list," I say. "Some kind of sinister *to-do* list."

Jonah sits back and pops an Oat Crunchie in his mouth. "Agreed. The words *bomb* and *Met* are obvious. *Test* has to be what the Fox was talking about.

But *plaza*? There are thousands of plazas in New York. And what about *tomb*? Grant's Tomb?"

"That fits. But what's going to happen at Grant's Tomb?" I rub my temples. Or does the word *tomb* have something to do with the Angel of Death painting?

The front door of our apartment opens. "I'm back!" Mom calls.

What? So soon? Glancing at the clock, I realize more than three hours have passed and the carnival's going to start in an hour. Once again I haven't done my homework.

Quickly Jonah and I fold up our notes and stuff the list into his backpack. "This is huge," he says. "We know that Lars, or the Fox or whoever it is, is going to strike at a plaza and a tomb. And that person is *definitely* going to rob the Met. I know we'll get in trouble for hacking into Bovano's computer, but we have to tell him about this."

I replay the words over and over again in my mind. *Bomb, test, plaza, Met, tomb.* I don't trust any of this. Maybe Jonah's right: maybe Lars, a.k.a. the Fox, is distracting me with texts about old gold while he sets his sights on the Met. What else could it be?

"We'll tell Bovano today," I say. "But let's do it after the carnival. If we tell him now, he won't do Frank's Tank, and Milton's counting on that as a big moneymaker." I figure I owe Milton for all his help.

Besides, once we tell Bovano, then it's all over. He'll kick me off the case and tell my parents about the hack, and they'll ground me for life. I need to figure out what *plaza* and *tomb* mean before then. I look at my watch. We have five hours to solve the unsolvable.

Chapter 17

BANSHEE

2:55 P.M., SAME DAY

"Three rings for a dollar," I call out. I wave a yellow plastic ring in the air. My ring toss booth consists of a table, three rows of five wooden pegs, and three plastic rings. I also have a bag of tiny prizes for the winners, including plastic spiders and pirate tattoos. I've made more than forty dollars. Not half bad, considering my sneezes are driving away potential customers.

My shift is almost over. Only two more hours until I tell Bovano about the list. I still haven't come up with any theories about the plaza *or* the tomb.

Jonah is two booths down from me at the bottle cap station, a pretty lame game of throwing bottle caps into small cups. Mostly he drums on the cups with pencils.

Paula is helping out at the lemonade stand and

Detective Bovano is in Frank's Tank. When he went down into the water for the first time, I expected him to come up spluttering and angry, but he laughed. I'd never heard him truly laugh. It was a pleasant sound, a deep belly laugh that made people smile.

I see Milton join Jonah at the bottle cap booth. They talk for a moment, and then Jonah grins, gives him a thumbs-up, and heads in my direction.

"I'm done," he announces. "Ready?"

I shake my head. "Not yet. I can't leave until Ryan shows up to take the next shift. Knowing him, he'll be late." I look around to make sure no one's listening. "We need to talk," I say. Then I frown. Those are the exact words Bovano said to me the other day. Maybe Paula's right—maybe I *am* turning into Frank Junior.

"Roger that." Jonah hops back and forth, the curly hair bouncing on his head. He's wearing a *Walter the Flying Cow* T-shirt that has suspicious red stains on it. He'll be wired on fruit punch for hours.

Suddenly he stops moving. His eyes widen at something behind me. "I'll be by the cotton candy," he says. "I'm there if you need me." With a spazzy hop-step, he turns and half walks, half dances away.

I turn to see Ryan James approaching my booth, along with . . . Jenny Miller.

"Hey, Edmund," Ryan says. "How's business?"

"Good. Forty-three bucks so far." I hand him the money, along with the bag full of prizes. "Have fun."

Jenny smiles a shy smile at me. Today she's wearing a dark blue Japanese kimono and chopsticks in her hair. "Want to walk around?" she asks.

"Okay." I stuff my hands in my pockets, my pulse thrumming in my ears. We wind our way between the booths and I try not to trip over my own feet. *Act normal. Make normal conversation.* "Do you want something to eat?"

She shakes her head. To our left, Ron Wibbey throws a ball at the dunk tank lever and nails the target with a sharp thwack. Mr. Frank is dunked in the water again. The crowd cheers and Jenny and I laugh. I get a whiff of my breath. Why did I eat a hot dog covered in onions an hour ago? What was I thinking? And I have a cold . . . what if I sneeze on her?

We fall silent again. I spot Jonah over by the cotton candy. He gives me a subtle thumbs-up. There's a reason he's been my best friend since we were two: greatest wingman ever.

"Do you want to check out the maze?" Jenny asks. "My mom's in there dressed as a banshee. She really went all out for it, with a black cape and fake blood."

This year the parents decided to make a haunted maze with zombies, vampires, and apparently banshees. There's a wooden entrance that looks like a coffin, and then rows of hay bales and white sheets that block the outside view. It must be pretty funny and scary, because I've heard a lot of screams and laughter all afternoon.

"Sure." I'm not really a huge fan of Halloween stuff, but I don't want to seem like a party pooper.

We head through the wooden coffin door and past a wall of mirrors. Silly cackling laughter and hoots play on a recording around us. My ears are clogged from my cold, throwing my senses off. Jenny grabs my hand, tugging me around the corner to where the maze begins. She lets go but I can still feel her palm on mine.

We come to an intersection. Left or right? She motions me left. "I think it's this way," she says. We step onto a path that's lined on either side by white sheets. The sheets sway and billow in the wind, making it difficult to see which way we're supposed to go next.

She speeds up and I follow, but I'm distracted. I

need to ask her about the stupid dance, once and for all. I'll do it as soon as we get out of here. No more wimping out.

Jenny's gone on ahead without me. I can hear her laugh but can't see her with all the rows of sheets. My knee bumps into a hay bale. I know this is part of the "maze experience," but I really don't like stumbling around disoriented.

The hairs on my neck prickle. Someone's behind me. There's a rustle and a flash of black. "Mrs. Miller?" I call out. Jenny said her mom was wearing a black cape. I don't want her to screech in my face. My hands are out in front of me as I try to push through the wall of sheets.

"Here, kitty, kitty," a voice murmurs.

I open my mouth to scream but strong arms jerk me off my feet and a damp cloth is shoved over my nose and lips. Sharp chemical vapors sting my eyes. "Night, night," the voice whispers in my ear.

A voice that has a thick German accent.

Chapter 18

TAKING STOCK

4:55 P.M., SAME DAY

Thirty minutes ago I woke up in a hotel bedroom. A really, *really* nice hotel bedroom, complete with silky sheets, super-soft pillows, and expensive artwork on the wall. Judging from the open duffel beside my bed, Lars must have drugged me, stuffed me in a bag, thrown me over his shoulder, and walked right out of the carnival maze and into a waiting car. Apparently my body's the size of five soccer balls.

My parents must be frantic. Jonah must be flipping out completely, calling everyone he knows to try to mount some kind of attack. I take deep, calming breaths through my nose, promising myself that I will return home to them safely. My hands won't stop shaking.

As far as I can tell, there are four men holding me captive. Lars, of course, is their leader. I knew he wasn't stupid enough to get blown up in Germany. Then there are two guys who are clearly the hired muscle. I know them—they're Snaggle and Rock, the same guys that Bovano showed me a few weeks ago in the surveillance van, the ones I suspected stole the crown.

O'Malley Junior is the fourth in their gang. That's right, O'Malley the Indian guy from the Met. I knew he and Lars were working together! Why doesn't Bovano ever listen to me?

My throat is sore and my head hurts. Lars informed me that I was experiencing side effects from the chloroform I breathed in. Then he offered me a glass of orange juice. I thought he was trying to poison me, and he got really mad when I wouldn't drink it. Finally O'Malley convinced me that the juice was fine after he took a sip.

I examine my room for the millionth time, searching for a way to escape. We're in the famous Plaza, one of the most expensive hotels in the city. At first I tried to be all clever and look out my window to pinpoint exactly where I was, but then I saw a notepad on the side table that said PLAZA HOTEL, so I guess Lars isn't trying to keep our whereabouts a secret.

I used the notepad to make HELP ME signs and

stuck them in the window, but we're at least five floors up, and no one can see me down on the street. I also drew pictures of the bad guys and wrote a *Help me, I've been kidnapped by these men* note. My plan is to fold the paper into an airplane and shoot it out into the hotel hallway when one of them opens the outer door. I wanted to send it out the window, but all of the glass panes are sealed shut.

"Dinner's ready, kitty," Lars says from the doorway. With his thick accent, I can't tell if he's calling me *kitty* or *kiddy*. Both nicknames are creepy.

He's changed his appearance once again. He's got long black hair pulled into a ponytail, a trimmed black beard, and dark eyebrows plucked into high thin lines. He looks like a weird bearded lady who will most likely haunt my nightmares for the rest of my life.

I admit that when I first woke up and met Lars face-to-face, I kind of freaked out and started hyperventilating. Imagine meeting a famous person who you've thought about nonstop for the past year. Now imagine that famous person is very cunning and evil and is holding you prisoner. It wasn't a pretty sight, but I got myself under control quickly. First rule of combat: Show no weakness.

Help me, I've been kidnapped by these men

I get off the bed and follow him into a living room, where two plush striped sofas sit near an enormous television. In the corner there's a marble bust of a man (probably stolen), wearing the Duchess of Ireland's emerald and diamond crown (*definitely* stolen). I make a silent vow to return it safely to her.

Strangest of all are the clocks. They're everywhere: on tables, hanging from walls, resting on chairs. Some are digital, some the old-fashioned wind-up. They all read different times, even crazy times like 78:21.

We enter a small kitchenette. O'Malley is by himself, eating at the table. He points to the spot beside him and I sit down to a plate of herbed chicken and mashed potatoes swimming in butter. It smells really good. O'Malley takes a quick bite of my potatoes to show me they're safe, and smiles.

Not only do they want to keep me alive, but they're actually treating me well. The food looks delicious, they've offered me any pay-per-view movie I want, and I even get an iPad to play video games (Internet service disconnected, of course).

It all leads to the biggest question in this whole nightmare. What do they want from me?

I sneeze and Lars recoils. He nervously squirts disinfectant on his hands. Note to self: Lars is a germa-phobe. Maybe I can use that to my advantage.

Despite the trauma of being kidnapped, I'm starving. I take a bite of chicken. Chew. Swallow. It's the best chicken I've ever tasted. I can't help myself—I take another bite.

You would think I'd be crying and completely hysterical about being kidnapped. I *am* nervous, but I'm also strangely calm. Maybe I'm in shock, but I don't think so. I've outwitted Lars before, and I will do it again. So I watch. I observe. I study every last detail to try to plan my escape.

Lars takes the seat across from mine at the rectangular table. Rock sits to my right. I'm not sure where Snaggle is. The suite we're in is pretty big. I've counted four bedrooms, a small kitchen, a dining room, and a living room.

"So this is your new Picasso Gang?" I say to Lars, waving my fork at the other men.

"No. There is only one Picasso Gang." He sits back in his chair and looks me up and down. "I would call this my *Eddie* Gang. In honor of our most valuable guest." He strokes his dark beard. "Although you are much shorter up close than I thought you'd be."

I ignore the comment and take another bite of chicken. Chew, chew, chew, swallow. "Why'd you steal the crown?" I ask. "Was it just to get my attention? I thought you only steal art."

He smiles, the skin by his mouth pulling tight like Saran Wrap from all the plastic surgery he's had. "I had to make the police nervous. That was the only way they'd send you to the Met, is it not?"

I nod, although I have no idea what he's talking about. Why would he need *me* at the Met?

"And I love jewels," he adds. "I have quite a large collection at home." His smile widens as if to say *By large collection, I mean Major Stolen Goods.*

I'm losing my appetite, but I move on to the mashed potatoes and take a bite. My hand trembles. Usually Jonah's military tactics march through my brain when I'm in a stressful situation, but it's Milton's voice I hear as I plan my survival strategy. Making lists is very soothing, and I wonder if this is why Milton speaks the way he does. I review everything I have going for me in a plan of action:

1. There are no hotel phones, but each bad guy has a cell. Keep track of all cell phones. Wait until

they are asleep, then grab a phone and call the police.

2. Pay attention to the hotel workers. They will come by to clean or deliver food. Find a way to be in the room when they do.

3. Sneeze often. Lars is nervous about germs. Nervous equals distracted equals opportunities for escape.

4. O'Malley keeps himself apart from the others, as if he's not one of the gang. Could he be an ally?

5. Use your pepper pen.

Yes, I have the pepper pen Jonah gave me. I have a weapon. Lars must have searched my pockets when I was passed out, because when I woke up I found my pocketknife was gone, along with my cell phone. But he left the pen because it looks like a dumb, harmless pen. I only get one shot, so I'll have to make it count.

"I need to see the inside," Lars is saying. "We have no access to the basement. That is why I sent O'Malley dressed as a guard. I knew you would see him, just as I knew the police would send you to the basement. So now you . . . you are our camera."

He looks at me as if he expects a response. The silence is filled with the steady *tick tick tick* of three clocks on the counter. My forehead wrinkles. "Uh . . ." I begin.

He gives an impatient stomp of his foot. "You tell me where they are in storage, eh? You do this." He slaps down a piece of paper and a pen. "Draw," he demands.

I stare at the paper. "Draw what?"

He makes a disgusted noise in his throat, as if I'm the stupidest person he's ever met. "The rooms. Security cameras, ceiling ducts, exits. Everything." He points to the paper. "Draw," he repeats.

Understanding washes over me like the cold water from Frank's Tank. This has nothing to do with lost gold from the Civil War or Alexander Fox's treasure exhibit at the Smithsonian. I am a camera. Lars's camera. He said I was next.

And now he wants me to help him rob the Met.

Chapter 19

RETIREMENT

─────

FIVE SECONDS LATER

"I can't remember." I stare at the puddle of melted butter on my plate, all that remains of my dinner.

Lars takes out a large pocketknife, flips open a particularly sharp and shiny blade, and begins cleaning his nails with it. "Are you sure?"

I grip the sides of my chair. *Play it cool. He won't hurt you if he thinks you can help him.* I nod. "I'm nervous. And I don't feel well." I sniffle to illustrate my point. "Maybe in a few hours my memory will come back. It does that."

"We don't have a few hours," he says. "What a pity." He nods to Rock, who stands up and comes behind my chair. Is he going to kill me right here, right now?

Suddenly I have an idea. I let out a little moan. "I have a really bad cold," I explain. Then I sneeze.

Instead of reaching for a tissue, I wipe my nose with my sleeve. Gross but effective. Lars squirms as if I've placed a spider on the table. "My memory gets messed up when I'm sick. There's only one thing that will make me feel better quickly. Wonton soup with no wonton, from Madame Ling's Chinese restaurant."

Lars frowns. "Chicken is best for a cold. Chicken and potatoes." He gestures to my empty plate.

"It's a really special soup with healing herbs. And they have gluten-free lo mein noodles." I add this last part for O'Malley's benefit. I heard him talking on the phone to room service when they messed up his sandwich order. He has celiac disease and can only eat gluten-free foods. "The restaurant is on Columbus and West Seventieth. Not far from here."

O'Malley, who up until now has been very quiet, turns to Lars and says, "I'll get it, yeah? I've not had lo mein in years."

Lars looks at me, then at O'Malley. "We will order delivery," he says coolly. "Just to the lobby, not the room." Then he turns back to me. "Okay, kitty. We will get you your soup. But if this is a trick . . ." He holds the knife up to the side of his eye.

I swallow hard. "No, sir," I say. "The soup will really help me."

He nods and then points to the piece of paper with his blade. "Then you draw."

An hour later I have a bowl of Madame Ling's wonton soup (without the wonton) and three perfectly drawn maps of the Met's storage facility. I also wrote out a detailed list of where the different Picassos are stored. Lars is happy. Snaggle is happy. Rock looks like he's ready to kill someone, but maybe he always looks like that. O'Malley is sitting quietly on the sofa, hugging his bowl of gluten-free lo mein noodles to his chest.

Here's my plan: According to Madame Ling, I'm the only person in the city who likes wonton soup without the wonton. So if O'Malley called it in to be delivered to the Plaza, Madame Ling would check in with my mom to ask what we're doing at the Plaza Hotel (she's good friends with my mom, since we eat at her restaurant so much). Mom will talk to Jonah, who will understand it's a message from me. He'll realize that *plaza* on the list means Plaza Hotel. He'll call Bovano, who will actually listen to him. And then they'll come and rescue me.

It's a long shot, but it's all I have to hold on to.

I clear my throat to get Lars's attention. He looks up from the plans I've drawn, staring at me with ice-cold eyes. I know I shouldn't engage him in conversation, but I'm dying to understand how the past few weeks all fit together. "If you've been after the Met this whole time," I say, "then why'd you send me those texts? Why aren't you robbing the Smithsonian and the old gold, like you said? Why call yourself the Fox?"

He smirks. "That was my associate. She handles the technology. The Smithsonian means nothing. You passed her test, that was all."

She? I open my mouth but he cuts me off.

"No more questions." He gestures to Rock, who escorts me down the hallway to my bedroom. I close the door and press my ear against the wood. I hear a lot of rustling noises, followed by German spoken in low tones. A key rattles in the front door. There are no bolts on the door, only a keyhole. I need to get my hands on that key. The door of the suite opens and closes, and a lock clicks into place. I peek out of my room.

"It's just you and me, lad," O'Malley calls from down the hall. He has a slight accent. "Come watch the telly," he adds. "I won't hurt you."

I find him on the couch, twisting wires in the back of a clock. A bag of white clay is on the table in front of him. I have a feeling it's a real explosive this time and not flour mixed with water.

He stops and wipes his fingers on a rag, then extends his hand to shake mine. "I'm Rajani O'Malley. You can call me Raj. Have a seat." He points to the couch across from his.

I sit down. "I'm Eddie Red. But you can call me Edmund."

He nods and gets back to work. Four other bombs are on a side table next to the wall. They're all blinking the same time of 13:38. A minute passes and suddenly they all read 13:37. They're counting backwards. Thirteen hours until they explode? I glance at my watch. That will be exactly nine o'clock tomorrow morning, when a lot of families are out for their Sunday stroll, enjoying the monuments. The thought sickens me.

"You seem like a nice person, Raj. Why are you doing this?" I motion to the bomb in his hands.

His expression darkens. "I got no choice. I'm a prisoner, same as you."

"You went to the lobby for Chinese food," I say. "You could run."

He snorts. "No one runs from Lars, no one hides from Lars. Surely you of all people can appreciate that." He rakes a hand over his short black hair. "Last year my father double-crossed Lars. A month later dear old Dad was thrown in a Russian prison, so I'm the unlucky bloke who's got to pay his debt."

A commercial comes on for Cheesy Crunchers, Jonah's favorite potato chip. Sadness floods my chest. I wonder what Jonah's doing right now. He must be really upset. I try to send him telepathic messages: *I'm safe . . . stay calm . . . tell Bovano to come get me at the Plaza Hotel . . .*

"I tried to warn you," O'Malley suddenly says. "I stood by that painting in the Met so you would understand what was coming for you."

"The Angel of Death?" I squeak. "Is Lars going to kill me?"

"Blimey, no," he says hurriedly. "It was a metaphor. Evil was coming for you. I . . . look, just forget it. What's done is done." He mutters something under his breath and picks up a small pair of pliers from the toolbox beside him.

He tried to warn me. He must hate Lars as much as I do. The enemy of my enemy is my friend. "Lars seems pretty pleased with his Met plan. He's been after Picassos this whole time?"

"Don't forget about the diamonds, yeah? The royal exhibit coming to town. It's a one-two punch. Crime of the century."

"The jewels are already at the Met?" Mentally I curse Bovano for not telling me this information. "I thought the exhibit was next month."

He nods. "The diamonds arrived early. They're in storage." He pulls out a spool of red wire. "Usually I make the cut-wire green, but this time I'll do it in red. For you." He gestures to my red hat with his pocketknife. "I'll do three in red. The cut-wire's the middle one, but loops left at the end." He snips the wire and my heart skips a beat. I can't believe I'm sitting here chatting with a man who could blow us to bits with one wrong move. He's calm and barely paying attention as his fingers work.

"Do you do this for a living?" I ask.

"No. I was third year at university when Lars found me. I'm studying to be a teacher like my mum. This"—he waves the pliers at the bombs on the table—"is a skill I picked up from Dad. Some kids play cricket with their father. Mine taught me how to rig a bomb."

He studies the weapon of destruction in his hands.

"This bomb triggers the others," he explains. "It will blow at Grant's Tomb, then set off the rest of them in a chain reaction around the city: Wall Street, the Brooklyn Bridge, Rockefeller Center, Grand Central. But if it's stopped in time, none of them will blow." He doesn't look at me as he speaks. Why is he telling me this?

And the Brooklyn Bridge? What does that have to do with anything? "What about the other landmarks?" I say. "The William Sherman statue and Cleopatra's Needle?"

"Decoys. Lars wants to strike high-traffic areas. It's his final farewell to the city, and a punishment to the NYPD for stopping him last time." With a final twist of wire and a snap of plastic, he closes the back of the bomb. Stretching his arms, he says, "I'm hungry. Do you want more soup? I bought you two containers."

"Okay."

We decide to watch a reality show about racecar drivers. It's really not my thing, but whatever makes him happy and relaxed. I ask if I can doodle on some paper and he gets me a notepad and pencil. I sketch the different rooms in the hotel suite, hoping to catch a detail I might have missed, a hiding place for a key or a cell phone. Meanwhile Raj tells me stories about

university and how he met a woman he really likes but is too nervous to ask out.

I smile and nod and keep drawing the rooms. *Where are you hiding that key, Lars?*

I wait.

And wait.

And wait.

Jonah doesn't come. The police don't come. I am still on my own. I need a plan B, but my brain is exhausted and a headache is pounding in my skull. I could spray O'Malley with the pepper pen and try to flee, but without a key, I can't unlock the door. I'm trapped.

I rub the back of my neck. I still don't understand Lars's comment about the Fox. "Raj," I say, "who is the Fox? Lars said something about his associate. He used the word 'she.'"

He shrugs. "Don't know. He doesn't tell me much. I just do what I'm told or he'll kill my mum."

"Oh." When he puts it that way, I guess I can't blame him for making these terrible bombs.

An hour later, the door to the suite opens. Lars, Rock, and Snaggle stride through. Lars drops a heavy red velvet bag on the table that makes a clinking noise. Fishing a hand inside the bag, he pulls out a crown with a brilliant white diamond the size of my fist and tosses it to O'Malley. Then he pulls out four rolled-up canvases from a long leather case and lovingly places them on the coffee table. I catch a glimpse of one. I recognize it as a beautiful Picasso in bold reds and yellows.

Lars grins and slaps his hands together. "Gentlemen, now we retire!"

I wish *I* had retired from being Eddie Red oh, about twenty-four hours ago.

I put my head in my hands. I just assisted in the crime of the century. Will I go to prison for this? A small blue velvet bag lands on the couch beside me. "For you, kitty," Lars says.

Against my better judgment, I peek inside. Diamonds, at least a hundred of them. I bet they could pay for the rest of my years at Senate, plus college, plus an apartment on Park Avenue.

"Thanks," I say in a tight voice. I put the bag on the coffee table. Does he really think I'd take them?

Lars raises his eyebrows at my actions but says nothing. He and his men head to the kitchen for a late-night snack. My gaze flickers over to O'Malley, who's fiddling with his new crown and watching me with a dark stare.

"I can go home now, right?" I say.

He smiles, but it doesn't reach his eyes. "Sure, lad. Tomorrow."

Chapter 20

THE HORSE

8:11 A.M., SUNDAY

I try not to sleep. I stare at the crazy digital clock in my room that reads 52:15 and never changes time. Eventually I must pass out, because I wake up in a puddle of drool. Ironically, my cold feels better. My watch says 8:11 a.m. Less than an hour until the bombs go off.

O'Malley appears in the doorway. "Breakfast," he says. He looks terrible, with dark shadows under his eyes as if he didn't sleep at all last night.

As I follow him out of the room, a potted plant in the front hall snags my attention. It's been shifted to the left by three inches. Yesterday it was lined up perfectly beneath a painting, but now it's off-center. Someone moved it. Is that where they keep the key?

We turn the corner and head into the living room.

The bags of jewels and the Picassos are gone, along with my bag of diamonds. And the bombs aren't on the table anymore. They must already be in place at the landmarks.

"Where's Lars?" I ask. Snaggle and Rock are standing by the windows, but Lars is nowhere to be seen.

"He left for Europe this morning," O'Malley says. He won't look me in the eye. Something's wrong. Very, very wrong.

"There's a huge horse outside," Snaggle grunts.

O'Malley frowns and walks over to the window, motioning for me to follow. As we approach, I hear loud trumpets and thumping drums. A parade?

I peer out the glass. My heart stutters. Senate Academy Middle School is marching down the street! The brown Trojan horse is on a truck bed, surrounded by kids dressed in Greek costumes, who are waving from the float. Some kids are playing musical instruments, while others hold *Walter the Flying Cow* balloons. The balloons are a personal message from Jonah — they *have* to be. He found me! He found me and he's coming for me!

I glance at O'Malley. He looks from me to the horse, back to me again. His mouth opens and closes as if he wants to say something but is too scared. He's making me really nervous. I need to get out of here.

"I need to use the bathroom," I announce.

"I'll take him." Rock's voice is raspy like sandpaper. It's the first time I've heard him speak. O'Malley nods, staring down at the carpet. Rock walks me back down the hall toward my bedroom. I reach into my pocket and flip the pepper pen to the "on" position.

"You should have taken the diamonds, kid," he says. "You failed his final test." He reaches a hand into his back pocket and pulls out a gun.

Quickly I bring my arm up and spray the mace right in his eyes. He stumbles away from me, dropping the gun and screaming while clutching his face. With panicked movements, I dive for the potted plant and look behind it, searching, searching . . . yes! My fist closes around a small key. I run to the door, shove the key into the keyhole, and twist. Freedom!

As I swing open the door and race into the outside hall, I glance over my shoulder. O'Malley appears by the potted plant, with Snaggle close on his heels. Snaggle sees me escaping and starts to lunge forward, but O'Malley grabs him around the waist. "Go!" he shouts at me. "Run!"

There's no time to wait for an elevator. I heave my shoulder into the emergency exit door and sprint down the stairwell, my feet barely touching the steps.

One flight, two flights, three. I run and run. Are there footsteps behind me? I can't tell and I don't dare stop to listen. Finally I reach the bottom and push through a heavy door. Sunlight blinds me as I step out into a side alley. *Keep running!*

I stumble toward the street. A crowd has gathered on the sidewalk, clapping and cheering. About thirty feet away, two policemen are directing the Trojan horse down a side street and away from the hotel. Jonah's nowhere to be seen. I need to find Paula and Bovano immediately. We need to stop that bomb!

The crowd is thick. I search for a familiar face from the precinct, and then I see it: a white van with FRANK'S FLOWERS on the side, parked down the block. Paula's on the sidewalk beside the van, talking to a group of men. Her back is turned to me so she doesn't see me approach.

"We believe the package is in room four twenty-two," she's saying. "We'll move in tactical teams of two. On my count, we'll—"

"Paula!" I yank on her shirt like an excited little kid.

She turns around and shuffles back a step. "Edmund?" she says in disbelief. Then "Edmund!" she shouts, and grabs me in a fierce hug. "How did you . . . ? Never mind, we'll talk in the car. Get in." She opens the front of the van for me, but I stay where I am.

"Lars is at the airport," I say. "He's there right now, heading for Europe. The other bad guys are still in the hotel. There are three of them. And there's a bomb set to blow at Grant's Tomb. We have to stop it or it will trigger bombs all over the city."

She stares at me. I think she's going to shut me down like Bovano always does, but instead she barks new orders at her men while pointing for me to get into the van. This time I do. She climbs into the driver's seat, a cell phone by her ear.

"Big Red is secure," she says into the phone. She guns the engine and pulls us into traffic. "Yes, he's okay. We need a team at the airport. Heinrich is there. International flights. Yep. We need a bomb squad at Grant's Tomb. I'll deliver Big Red to the precinct and—"

"We can't go to the precinct," I interrupt. "Are you talking to Bovano? Tell him I know how to diffuse the bomb. O'Malley made it different from the others. The cut-wire isn't green — it's red!"

She frowns and says into the cell, "Did you catch that?"

I can hear Bovano's gruff voice on the other end, but I can't hear what he's saying. Paula pauses, then says, "Frank, we're on our way. There's still time. Yes, I'm bringing him. We'll stay in the van, away from the blast zone. Don't cut until we get there!" She hangs up and tosses the phone into her purse. "There's still time," she repeats to me. "Frank is en route to Grant's Tomb. We'll meet him there." She rolls down her window and slaps a red strobe light on the roof of the van. A siren blares and cars start to pull over in front of us.

I look at my watch. Twenty-five minutes until the bomb explodes. Yes, there's time, but not much. We still have to deal with New York City's traffic.

"Hang on!" Paula shouts. She speeds up, weaving from lane to lane, honking the horn if people don't move fast enough.

I clutch my door as we race through three intersections. We're approaching Amsterdam Avenue. "Take a right here," I say, but she's already doing it.

"I know." She yanks the wheel. "I studied that map you gave me."

We drive on, the siren blaring in my ears. "Hey, Paula," I yell over the wailing noise.

"Yeah?"

"Thanks for changing my code name."

Chapter 21

BOOM AT THE TOMB

A FEW MINUTES LATER

The streets are a blur of people clutching coffee cups while walking their dogs and pushing baby strollers. With a screech of tires, Paula makes a sharp left turn and pulls onto the curb, the van bouncing all over the place. We come to a shuddering stop and I realize we're a few hundred feet down the road from Grant's Tomb. Her phone rings. Quickly she talks with Bovano, then hangs up.

She kills the engine. "Frank's already inside. He said it's a small bomb. He's got a camera that's linked to a monitor here." She points to the back of the van. "The closer we are, the clearer the picture." Opening the partition to the back of the van, she gestures with her head. "Let's go."

I scramble into the back and sit in the chair where

Bovano usually sits. My watch reads 8:52. Eight minutes left.

Paula puts on a headset and I follow suit. Quickly she shows me the buttons that zoom the picture in and out, left and right. "Frank?" she says into the headset. "We're here and in position."

"Copy." Bovano's voice is loud in my ears. Suddenly his face appears on the monitor in front of me. A black-and-white monitor. "Eddie?"

"I'm here." My heart is pounding in my ears. How are we going to do this with a black-and-white screen? How can I tell the red wires from the green?

"Glad you're okay," he says. He clears his throat. "Here's the bomb." He shifts the camera and the bomb comes into view. He's made a mess of the wires, the orderly rows of green and red now pulled into a tangled clump. The flashing numbers on the bomb read 6:52 . . . 6:51 . . .

"It's usually the fifth green wire," he says. "Lucky number five. Only . . ."

"Only this bomb is different," I say, moving closer to the screen. My nose is practically touching the glass when I realize I can press a button and zoom the camera lens in closer. "I saw O'Malley put it together. It's the middle red wire, red for Eddie Red."

"You're sure?" Bovano asks. "I have a bomb squad here who can move it to the Hudson River. The water should contain the blast."

"If it blows, it will set off other bombs around the city," I explain. "We *have* to diffuse it."

"Hold this," he says to someone. The camera bounces around and a knife comes into view, along with Bovano's stout fingers. "This is the middle red wire," he says, holding up a wire. "There are two more—here, and here." He points to two other wires.

Sweat beads on my neck and face. From where I'm sitting, all the wires are the same shade of gray. When I don't respond, he slides his knife beneath that middle wire.

"Wait," I say. Something's not right. O'Malley said the red wire started in the middle and looped left. This red wire starts in the middle but it seems to loop right. Is it the wrong wire, or has Bovano made such a tangled mess of things that it's impossible to tell?

Beside me, Paula starts to whisper. I think she's praying.

"Eddie, you've got to be kidding me!" Bovano's

voice is boiling with anger. "This is life or death, do you understand?"

I wipe the sweat off my forehead and close my eyes, envisioning the three red wires. The cut wire started in the center with the rest of them, wrapped around a coil of green, and then veered left, plunging into the back of the bomb. There's only one red wire that wraps around a bunch of green wires, and it's not the one he's holding.

Sixty seconds left. Fifty-nine. "It's the second one you pointed to," I say. "The one on the left."

There's silence on the other end. Bovano moves his blade away. "It's time to clear out," he says. "We've done all we can."

"Why don't you ever listen to me?" I yell. "When have I ever been wrong? When it really counts, I mean."

A heavy sigh fills my ears. Just as a wave of panic rolls over me, the knife comes back onto the screen. "Okay," he says. He shifts the blade so it rests beneath the new wire. "It's been nice working with you, Edmund," he says.

And cuts.

Chapter 22

FALLOUT

3:34 P.M., SUNDAY

My mother won't stop crying. And my father won't stop hugging me. The three of us are squished together on the couch in a parent-and-Edmund sandwich. "I'm okay, guys," I manage to wheeze. Dad's got me in a vise grip that has me struggling for air.

"We have to leave the city," Mom says in a thick voice. "They'll be coming for you."

I'm not sure who *they* is in her imagination. "The police caught the whole gang," I say against Dad's shoulder. "Lars, O'Malley, and the others. They'll be in jail for a long time. We're safe."

After we stopped the bomb, Paula and Bovano whisked me to the precinct for a debriefing. They told me all of the stolen goods were recovered, including the artwork from the Met and the duchess's diamond crown. There was no talk of reward money, but Chief Williams promised he'd give me a special award for my bravery. He also gave me his cell phone number and told me to call day or night if I had an emergency. I think my mother's meltdown qualifies, so I called him twenty minutes ago. He said he'd be right over to calm her down. She likes him and I think she'll listen to him.

Mom rubs her tired eyes. "I don't know what to do. I need time to think. We'll go to New Jersey, stay at Grandma's for a while. You can go to school there." As she speaks, her voice tapers off. She knows this is a ridiculous plan. She works in the city and just got promoted to senior agent at her real estate firm. She *can't* leave.

Finally I wiggle out of my father's arms and stand to face them. "Dad, tell her! There are no more bad guys! We won!"

He stares at me as if I might vanish any second. "We thought we lost you," he whispers.

"Those men could have friends," Mom says. "People you don't know about. Criminals stick together, they form alliances."

A knock sounds on the door. "That's Chief Williams," I say. "He wanted to talk to you personally, to reassure you that I'm safe."

"You don't know if that's him," Mom hisses. "Use the peephole, use the peephole!" I've never seen her like this. I need to put the brakes on the Motherly Panic, *immediately*.

I open the door (after using the peephole and confirming that it is, in fact, Chief Williams) and am tempted to throw myself into his arms. Finally a sane person has come to rescue me from freaked-out parents! Instead I shake his hand and thank him for coming. He nods in his grandfatherly way, and immediately takes charge of the situation, parking himself on the couch between my parents and speaking in a calm voice. He has Mom cracking a smile within two minutes. Once I'm sure that everything is under control, I excuse myself to go take a nap. I've spoken to enough police officers today.

My room is blissfully quiet, although it's a complete disaster. My desk drawer is open, papers are scattered on the floor, the pencil jar is tipped over, and there's a dried-up, half-eaten peanut butter sandwich on my dresser. Jonah Schwartz strikes again.

After I straighten up the mess, I lie down on my bed. I wish Jonah were here. I saw him at the precinct a few hours ago, grinning while being fingerprinted. They arrested him for the parade stunt he pulled. He was in a great mood, viewing his arrest as a badge of honor.

He said that when the cops realized I'd been kidnapped, they shut down the carnival and canceled the dance, claiming there had been a chemical spill on a nearby street. Nobody else knew I was gone.

Jonah knew. The moment he saw Paula's face, he knew what had happened. He went straight to my apartment and searched my room, reading my notes for any clues he might have missed. That's when Madame Ling called my mom. Jonah figured out what my Plaza message meant and told Bovano about it, who actually listened this time, although he ordered Jonah to stay away from the rescue operation.

Jonah wasn't going to take no for an answer. He thought a distraction might help with my escape, so he convinced our gym teacher, Mr. Reiner, that Senate was going to be part of one of those flash mobs on national TV. Mr. Reiner is gaga for flash mobs—and also not the sharpest tool in the shed—so he agreed to drive the float. Then Jonah told Milton that this was all a huge undercover operation for Bovano, so Milton helped round up a bunch of kids to do a "practice run" for Homecoming.

Bovano was pretty mad this morning at the station. There was a lot of yelling and scolding and threatening jail time. I came to Jonah's defense, claiming his horse decoy was instrumental in my escape. It's true. If it weren't for him, then Snaggle wouldn't have been so distracted. Who knows what would have happened.

In the end the cops decided not to charge Jonah with disturbing the peace *or* endangering the lives of children, but he may have to do some community service. He's also grounded for at least a month. Speaking of jail time, I feel bad that O'Malley was arrested as well. I told Bovano how O'Malley had let me go, and Bovano promised they'd go easy on him. Maybe I can visit him in jail and thank him personally for his help.

I take off my glasses and rub my face. I know I'm supposed to be resting, but my brain won't turn off and my eyes refuse to shut. I stand up and start to pace. One question remains: Who is the Fox?

It has to be someone I saw that day at the library. Someone who was watching me research lost treasure. I flip through images in my mind: the old man walking, the plump woman shelving books, the group of giggling kids. They were all busy doing other things when I received that first text. But the girl at the table . . . she had a magazine open and her hands were in her lap, hidden from view. Could she have been texting me? And now that I think about it, she walked behind me a few times while I was doing research.

A girl my age . . . *she's* the Fox? Why would she be working with Lars? Is she his daughter? Granddaughter? I didn't see much family resemblance, but Lars has had so much plastic surgery, who knows what he truly looks like.

A girl connected to Lars . . . and she's still out there, on the loose. Has she sent me any more texts? I grab my phone where it's charging on the nightstand. The police found it in the hotel room and returned it to me, but the batteries were dead so it's been charging for the past hour. I press the On button and the screen springs to life. There's one new text, sent this morning at 9:32 a.m. Just about the time Lars was being arrested at the airport.

I recognize the Fox's creepy 000–000–0000 number. With trembling fingers, I type in my password and a message pops up:

You ruined everything.

THE END?

HOW TO BE A CRYPTOGRAPHER

BY EDDIE RED

A cryptographer is a person who studies codes. There are tons of different kinds of codes out there. Some just use letters, some use numbers, and some use a combination of both. The one thing they have in common is that they need a key to unlock their meaning.

Staring at groups of numbers can be über-frustrating. For example, what could these numbers mean?

1 15 12   13 8 1   10 8 1

Each number represents a letter. But how to get started?

How do you figure out the key? There are a million tricks and complicated formulas that cryptographers use. Here are a few basic techniques that all good code crunchers should know:

1. Look for single-letter words. They are almost always *a* or *I*.
2. Look for two-letter words. They are almost always *of*, *to*, *in*, *on*, *is*, or *it*.
3. Look for repeating letter patterns. These words will probably rhyme.
4. Look for three-letter words. The most common are *the*, *and*, and *for*.

In the example above, there are three three-letter words, but the last two rhyme (the "8 1" pattern repeats). So those two words are probably not the word *the*. But could "1 15 12" be the word *the*? If $T = 1$, does $H = 15$? If $T = 1$, then $U = 2$, $V = 3$, and so on. So does $H = 15$? Yes! And if I plug in the rest of the letters into our code, I get this:

1	15	12		13	8	1		10	8	1
T	H	E		F	A	T		C	A	T

To try something trickier:
5 16 23   17 1   2 16 13   14 23 6?

It looks like a question. There are three three-letter words, one two-letter word, and no rhyming words. Could the first word be *the*? If $T = 5$, does $H = 16$?

No, H would be 19 in that case. Let's look at the two-letter word. Could it be the word *of*? If $O = 17$, does $F = 1$? No, F would be 8.

I'm going to stick with the short word since it has fewer letters. How about the word *is*? If $I = 17$, does $S = 1$? Yes, it does! We cracked the code. Assign all of the numbers letters, and you come up with this:

5 16 23   17 1   2 16 13   14 23 6?
W H O   I S   T H E   F O X?

Here's one last code:

8 15 23   4 15 5 19   12 1 18 19
11 14 15 23   20 8 5   6 15 24?

I spot three three-letter words and no rhymes. I guess we'll start with the first word. Could it be *the*? If $T = 8$, does

H = 15? No, it would be 22. How about the word "20 8 5" Could that be *the*? If *T* = 20, then yes, *H* = 8! We've cracked the code.

```
8  15  23      4  15  5  19      12  1  18  19
H  O   W       D  O   E  S       L   A  R   S
```

```
11  14  15  23      20  8  5      6  15  24?
K   N   O   W       T   H  E      F  O   X?
```

Good question—wouldn't I like to know. Here is my picture of the Fox. Be on the lookout—I have a feeling she's dangerous. Or at least very, very clever.

ACKNOWLEDGMENTS

Writing a book truly takes an enormous team effort. I would be completely lost without my Team Eddie. A huge thanks to my husband, Ben Wells, and my writing partner, Beth Charles, for reading and rereading countless versions of this story. To my editor, Ann Rider—thank you for your brilliant insights and your patience. To my agent, Kristin Nelson—thank you for swooping in and saving the day on this one!

A special thanks to my mom, Jeanne Williams, who is the founding member of the Eddie Red fan club, and whose love and support I lean on every day. Love you, Mom!

To my illustrator, the incredible Marcos Calo: *Muchas gracias por todo.*

Thank you, thank you, to my amazing team at Houghton Mifflin Harcourt: Scott Magoon, Mary Magrisso, Alison Kerr Miller, Candace Finn, Rachel Wasdyke, and all the other terrific folks who have helped Eddie along the way.

And finally to Riley and Allison, my family, my friends, and all the wonderful people I've met because of Eddie Red. I couldn't do this without you.

WITHDRAWN

31901059849473